pumpkin
spice up
your life

Also by Suzanne Nelson

Cake Pop Crush

You're Bacon Me Crazy

Macarons at Midnight

Hot Cocoa Hearts

Donut Go Breaking My Heart

Sundae My Prince Will Come

I Only Have Pies for You

Shake It Off

Serendipity's Footsteps

A Tale Magnolious

pumpkin
spice up
your life

Suzanne Nelson

SCHOLASTIC INC.

Copyright © 2020 by Suzanne Nelson
All photos © Shutterstock.com

Library of Congress Cataloging-in-Publication Data

Names: Nelson, Suzanne, 1976- author.
Title: Pumpkin spice up your life / Suzanne Nelson.
Description: New York : Scholastic Inc., 2020. | Audience: Ages 8-12. | Audience: Grades 4-6. | Summary: When her best friend Daniel concocts an elaborate plot to ask the new girl at school to the fall dance, Nadine realizes she has fallen for Daniel herself but fears she does not have the courage to tell him how she feels. Includes recipes.
Identifiers: LCCN 2020014132 | ISBN 9781338640489 (paperback) | ISBN 9781338640496 (ebook)
Subjects: CYAC: Coffeehouses—Fiction. | Best friends—Fiction. | Friendship—Fiction. | Dating (Social customs)—Fiction.
Classification: LCC PZ7.N43765 Pu 2020 | DDC [Fic]—dc23
LC record available at https://lccn.loc.gov/2020014132

10 9 8 7 6 5 4 3 2 1   20 21 22 23 24

Printed in the U.S.A.   40
First printing 2020

Book design by Jennifer Rinaldi

For the girls of
Ridgefield Troop 633,
who are not only my strong,
honest, and kind scouts but also some
of my most enthusiastic readers.

—S.N.

Chapter One

I opened the door to the Snug Mug, and a whirlwind of fiery red and orange leaves blew in with me. After shaking a few stragglers from my long, curly chestnut hair, I walked into our town's one and only coffee shop, like I did every day after school.

Shredder, the Bernese mountain dog who belonged to Marley, the Snug Mug's owner, was lazing in front of the roaring fireplace. I gave Shredder a hello ear scratch before tucking my cello case safely against the wall. My friend Elena Castillo was standing in line for coffee alongside her boyfriend, Brandon Jones, so I went to join them.

One look at the crush of customers ahead of us was all I needed to say aloud what I'd been feeling in the brisk air outside. "It's official. Fall has *definitely* arrived."

"Well, the leaf peepers certainly have." Elle shook her head at the camera-toting out-of-towners.

Nestled in our tree-steeped valley of Woodburn, Vermont, just a few miles from Killington ski resort, the Snug Mug was a draw for vacationing fall leaf peepers and winter skiers alike. But the rest of the year, it belonged almost entirely to us Woodburners. The Snug Mug was a decades-old log cabin turned coffee shop and gourmet waffle hut. With its creaky floorboards, woven rugs, and exposed overhead beams, it had a ramshackle coziness, and the blissful aromas of espresso and fresh-off-the-iron waffles added to the appeal.

And the best part of the Mug? My BFF, Daniel Dae Cho, worked behind the counter as a barista. At the moment, he was wowing a customer with his coffee art.

"It's a perfect leaf!" the out-of-towner declared. She gazed down happily at the foliage design Daniel had created in her

Flaming Fall Flat White. I felt a flush of pride on Daniel's behalf.

As the line inched forward, Brandon sighed, checking his phone. "Looks like we sold a record number of tickets to the Blaze," he reported, his freckled face dismayed.

The Big Pumpkin Blaze was a display of hand-carved jack-o'-lanterns in Woodburn's town park. Each night from October to the end of the November, the park was illuminated so people could walk its pathways, taking in its "gourd-geous" sculptures. It was our small town's biggest tourist draw. But Brandon was less than enthused about being one of the student volunteers who helped with the Blaze's nightly special effects. I, though, was excited for it; fall was my favorite time of year.

Elle gave Brandon a sympathetic smile. "A Heavenly Hazelnut Latte will cheer you up."

We reached the counter right then, and Daniel glanced up at us, grinning.

"Hey, Nadi!" he said. "Any sign of snow yet?"

"Don't even." I gave him a scolding look. "It's only October."

Daniel and Brandon always caught snowboarding fever at the first sign of frost. But couldn't they at least wait for the leaves to drop? I glanced from Daniel to Brandon. "You two powder hounds better not jinx us with snow before Saturday's fall festival."

"Powder hounds unite!" Daniel held an espresso portafilter aloft like a brandished sword while Brandon whooped in solidarity.

Marley, also behind the counter in his apron, nudged Daniel with an elbow. "Powder hounds make coffee." He raised a scolding eyebrow at Daniel as he poured espresso beans into the large silver brewer. Marley was like a surrogate uncle to Daniel, and he loved to razz him as they worked side by side.

"I'm on it, boss," Daniel said with his winning smile. Daniel had such a calming effect on anyone, he could've turned Jaws into a harmless guppy.

Marley chuckled. "I *do* actually need to talk to you, though, so let's chat once the line clears up."

I wondered what Marley needed to talk to Daniel about, but before I could ask, Daniel turned to me and said, "Your usual?"

"She never gets anything different." Elle ran one hand through her long, blue-tipped black hair while absently practicing her French horn fingering against her knee. Elle was petite, with long-lashed obsidian eyes and bronze skin that I envied. My own pale skin betrayed even the slightest blush, and turned fiery crimson whenever I was upset or angry. Fiercely smart, Elle was the first-chair French horn at our school, a force to be reckoned with when it came to her trills and multiphonics. "You know, Nadine, you *could* get something besides Daniel's Pumpkin Spice Supreme."

"It'll never happen." I was a die-hard creature of habit, and all my friends knew it. I couldn't practice my cello without first playing my favorite D- and A-note double stop. And I couldn't drink a Pumpkin Spice Supreme at the Snug Mug unless Daniel made it. In fact, Daniel had invented the Pumpkin Spice Supreme—a rich, creamy fusion of nutmeg, cinnamon, and pumpkin—just for me.

Daniel could brew some of the best coffee in Woodburn, but it had only been since the start of this school year that Marley had agreed to let Daniel help out at the Snug Mug every afternoon.

"You're always sneaking behind the counter to mix up some new coffee concoction whenever I turn my back anyway," Marley had told him with a laugh. Really, though, I suspected it was one of the unspoken ways Marley had of looking out for Daniel. Marley had been good friends with Daniel's dad way back when, and had a soft spot for Daniel because of it. Plus, lots of kids in Woodburn had unofficial jobs of one kind or another anyway, because most of the businesses here were family owned and operated.

And Daniel was a hit at the Snug Mug. His recipes were daring, outlandish, and fun. It had all started, though, with pumpkin spice.

"Pumpkin spice is so predictable," he'd told me on his first day as a barista, when I'd tried to order one. "*Everybody* drinks it *every* fall. And you are definitely *not* everybody. You deserve a one-of-a-kind drink for a one-of-a-kind Nadi." That had been a month ago, and since then, the Pumpkin Spice Supreme had become a local favorite.

Now, as Daniel steamed the milk and pumpkin puree together and poured them over the espresso in the special YOU HAD ME AT CELLO coffee mug he kept behind the counter for me, I thought back to how Daniel's coffee talent had begun.

I was in second grade when my mom left. She'd walked out the door with a blunt, "I want sidewalk cafés, cappuccinos, and grand adventures. *Not* being snowed in for seven months out of every year." After that, I became convinced that if I could learn to make a "cappu-whatever," I could get Mom back. Daniel, who'd lost his dad in a car accident when he was too little to remember, wanted to help. So, in his typical larger-than-life fashion, he decided we'd learn to make dozens of coffee drinks, to prepare for Mom's return. After school one day, we walked to the Snug Mug to ask Marley if he could teach us, and he agreed. In the end, though, it was Daniel who had developed the coffee talent, while I fell in love with the cello.

"Here you go," Daniel said now, squeezing a spiraling mountain of whipped cream atop my coffee. He added three anise seeds, a cinnamon stick, and a lacy sprinkling of cinnamon. "A one-of-a-kind drink for a one-of-a-kind Nadi."

"Why, thank you." I picked up the mug and breathed in the delicious scent of pumpkin, nutmeg, and cinnamon.

"Hey," Brandon teased. "How come Nadine got hers first? Where's my Heavenly Hazelnut? And Elle's Radical Raspberry Mocha?" He pulled an exaggerated pout while Elle laughed beside him.

"Patience is a virtue," Daniel said, his dark brown eyes sparkling as he got to work on the next order.

I took a slow, deep sip of my pumpkin spice latte. The taste made me think of hayrides, bonfires, and crisp autumn nights under winking stars. It made me think of Chopin's Cello Sonata, Opus 65, and the way playing it conjured images of flaming leaves trickling down from trees. "Mmm." I took a second sip. "It gets better every time." With my free hand, I reached into my book bag for my wallet, but, as always, Daniel waved me off.

"Stop," he said. "You know you guys are all VIP customers."

"Aw, thanks." I put my wallet back inside my bag and as I did, my thick daily planner fell out. Elle leaned down to pick it up.

She regarded my planner with a smirk. "Is there a 'Snug Mug hang time' reminder in here?" she asked. Elle liked to rib me about my so-called color-coded life, but I loved the rainbow of Post-its spanning my planner's pages—little "to-dos" I could pull off as I did them. "Or is there a Post-it for the Fall Formal? *If* you're actually going this year."

"Not likely." I grabbed the planner from her, laughing. "Daniel and I can't cancel our annual John Hughes movie marathon."

"Not a chance." Daniel grinned.

Daniel and I loved eighties movies, and we had skipped the last two years' formals in favor of our tradition. Daniel's favorite movie was *Ferris Bueller's Day Off*. Given the fact that Daniel had once skipped school to sneak onto the set of a movie being filmed at Killington, and actually ended up in a shot, he was doing a pretty good job of living like Ferris.

"Just you wait. I'm going to write *Fall Formal* on a Post-it and stick it in there." Elle jabbed a finger at my planner. "If the planner wills it, it shall be so."

"Hey. Don't knock the planner," I protested. "It's saved Daniel's neck a time or two." Not only did I keep track of *my* homework assignments and due dates, but Daniel's, too. I'd offered to start doing that after he'd turned in his third late project.

"True," Daniel said, smiling mischievously. "But sometimes you have to embrace the unexpected to suck the marrow out of life."

"I don't need to embrace anything right now except my bow in some serious practicing." I glanced at my cello case, feeling its pull even from half a dozen feet away.

Elle was about to respond when her phone rang. She stepped away to answer it, and I could tell by her switch from English into irritated Spanish that it was her youngest brother, Miguel, calling to complain about their older brother, Juan. Brandon stepped aside to put a soothing arm around her.

Daniel focused his gaze on me. Like always, he seemed to read my mind. "Stressing about your Interlochen audition already?"

"Already?" I repeated in disbelief. "The audition is in two weeks, and I still haven't decided on my final composition piece."

"Nadi, you were born ready for this audition." Daniel opened the mini fridge under the counter to get out a container of milk for Elle's drink. "You're the best cellist at our school!"

"Thanks, but that doesn't matter," I argued. "Kids from all over the country apply to the summer music camp program. The competition is *so* intense."

I'd dreamed of attending Interlochen Center for the Arts summer camp since sixth grade, when our school's orchestra director, Maestro Claudio, had given me a camp brochure. I wanted to be a professional cellist someday, and honing my skills at a fine arts school like Interlochen would help pave the way. First, though, I had to get accepted.

"I started a new composition today in orchestra." I pulled my phone out of my back pocket. "I recorded what I have so far." I took a deep breath. Daniel had never said no to hearing my new pieces, but asking him still made me nervous. Letting anyone listen to my compositions felt like baring my soul. "Want to listen?"

His hand, holding the portafilter full of pressed espresso grounds, paused. Then he smiled widely, and relief washed over me. This smile had won me over on the playground in kindergarten, when Daniel had invited me to make mud pies with him (he mashed the pies together while I organized them on a makeshift musical staff made of sticks). This smile had begun our friendship years ago and made me feel like we'd be friends forever. "Do I want to listen?" He locked the portafilter in place and set two espresso shot glasses underneath as the enticing, dark liquid streamed down. "Do I want to see the pyramids? Bike down Haleakala? Snorkel in the Great Barrier Reef?"

I laughed. Daniel was dying to do all of that, along with about a thousand other adventures on his bucket list. "Okay, okay. You want to hear it."

Just then, Marley appeared beside Daniel, cell phone in hand. "Hey, can you hold down the fort?" Marley asked. He was glancing out the front window at a sleek Range Rover that had just pulled into the parking lot. "I'll be back in a few." Daniel nodded, and Marley headed for the shop's door with Shredder close behind, tail wagging.

Brandon and Elle returned to the counter. Elle was grumbling about her brothers, but perked up when Daniel handed her a steaming cup of Radical Raspberry Mocha.

"Don't worry, your drink is up next," Daniel told Brandon before he could ask. Daniel rolled his eyes at me, deadpanning, "A genius's work is never done."

He grabbed another cup from the shelf and turned back to the espresso machine. Then he froze, staring past me toward the Snug Mug's front door, his jaw going slack.

"Daniel?" I said. "You okay?"

He nodded vaguely, but his eyes were fixed on the door. The cup in his hands slipped, shattering on the floor with an echoing crash. I hurried to help Daniel clean up the broken pieces, but he still hadn't moved. In fact, he seemed completely oblivious to the cup smashing and everything else. I nudged him gently.

"Daniel?" I whispered. "You're freaking me out. Blink if you can hear me." He blinked as his cheeks reddened. "Wha—" I started, but as I followed his gaze, I saw for myself.

In the doorway of the Snug Mug stood the most beautiful girl I'd ever seen. She had big brown eyes with long lashes, bow-shaped lips, and luminous brown skin set off by her purple hat and matching coat. She was gazing right at Daniel, who still hadn't moved, as if he was under the girl's spell.

Who was she, and what had she just done to my best friend?

Chapter Two

"Hey, Snug Muggers!" Marley called from the doorway. He stood beside the mystery girl and a tall, broad-shouldered man who was nearly as handsome as the girl was gorgeous. I guessed they were father and daughter. The man wore a dark dress coat that was out of place here among the hand-knitted sweaters and beanie caps of the Snug Mug customers.

"I—well, *we*—have an announcement to make." Marley glanced at the man and girl. "This is Mr. James Renaud and his daughter, Kiya. And . . . the Renauds are the new owners of the Snug Mug!"

Marley started applauding enthusiastically, and so did a hand-ful of out-of-towners who had no idea that this was, in fact, terrible news. From around the room came gasps and sad mut-terings of "What?" or "Why?" I glanced at Daniel in confusion, but my best friend was still staring at the new girl.

"I know it's a shock to some of you," Marley went on gently, "but I've been planning a 'rewirement' for a while." He leaned over to give Shredder a pat, and the dog let out a happy bark. "Shredder and I will always be Snug Muggers. I won't be behind the counter anymore, that's all. You'll be in great hands with the Renauds. They've moved up here from New York City, so let's give them a proper welcome." Marley then began walking the Renauds from table to table, introducing them.

"Can you believe it?" Elle asked. "Marley's owned the Mug since before we were born!"

"It's the end of an era," Brandon said forlornly.

"I know." I was gathering the broken pieces of the cup from the floor again. "Daniel, did Marley tell you about this?"

When Daniel didn't respond, I glanced up to find I

in a daze.

Brandon jerked his head toward Daniel and mouthed, *What's with him?*

"Kiya," Daniel muttered, not even noticing our presence. "What a beautiful name."

"Ooo-kay. Time to snap out of it." I dumped the ceramic pieces into the trash, then elbowed Daniel . . . *hard*.

"Ow!" he yelped in surprise. "What did you do that for?"

I cocked an eyebrow at him. "Because Marley just announced that he sold the Snug Mug and you're off in never-never land, that's why."

Daniel blinked, processing. "He . . . *what*?! How could he sell the Snug Mug?"

"*Thank you*. He's back! Finally!" I would've smiled in relief if I hadn't just heard that our favorite hangout was being sold to complete and total strangers.

At that moment, Marley glanced over worriedly, excused

himself from the Renauds, and hurried behind the counter. He clapped a hand on Daniel's shoulder. "Sorry to shock you, kiddo. I wanted to tell you before, but the Renauds got here early." He ruffled Daniel's hair. It was a gesture that showed how much Daniel meant to him, and spoke to how close they'd become in the years since Daniel's dad passed away. "Don't worry," Marley added. "Mr. Renaud's keeping you on. I've always got your back. We'll just have *our* hang time in front of the counter instead of behind it."

After a second's hesitation, Dan nodded. "And we'll still shred the gnar when the mountain opens?" he asked.

Marley laughed. "I wouldn't miss snowboarding with you for anything." Then he glanced toward the Renauds. "Right now, though, I better finish the obligatory intros."

"It sounds like it's a done deal already," I said after he walked away.

"This stinks." Daniel sighed.

"Yeah." Brandon nodded. "This new guy better be flexible. Otherwise, you can kiss your days of perpetual late-to-workness goodbye." He glanced at the remains of my Pumpkin Spice Supreme, which I hadn't finished because of the big news. "Hey, what happened to my order?"

Daniel slapped his forehead. "Oh man, I zoned. Sorry. My bad." He quickly set about making Brandon's Heavenly Hazelnut Latte. But as I walked back around the counter to finish my lukewarm drink, I noticed how distracted Daniel seemed. Every few seconds, he glanced up, scanning the room for Kiya. When she finally met his gaze and headed in our direction, Daniel's cheeks blushed anew.

"She's walking over," he whispered. There was a nervousness in his voice I'd never heard before.

Kiya was even prettier up close. She'd taken off her coat to reveal a stylish plum sweater and caramel suede leggings, and her hair, free of her hat, framed her face in tight dark brown coils. Every step she took exuded confidence, and her smile was open and friendly.

"You're Daniel," she stated when she reached the counter. "Marley said you're the Mug's best barista."

Daniel opened his mouth but no sound came out. Finally, he managed a nod as he set Brandon's Heavenly Hazelnut on the counter.

Kiya's smile widened, and even *Brandon* blushed, until Elle nudged him and stuck out her hand toward Kiya. "I'm Elle," she said. "This is my boyfriend, Brandon. And this is Nadine."

"Hi." I offered her a wave.

"It's so great to meet you all!" Kiya said enthusiastically. "I've been freaked out about starting school tomorrow. We don't know anyone here yet, so it will be such a relief to see some familiar faces in the hallways." She turned to Daniel. "And I'll be helping out here after school, so we'll be working together. But I have to warn you . . ." Her laugh was bell-like. "I don't know anything about coffee."

After a second's pause, Daniel at last found his voice. "No worries. When all else fails, just *brew* it." He emitted a high-pitched, awkward laugh. I exchanged confused looks with Elle and Brandon. Since when did Daniel make cringey jokes? I glanced at Kiya, fully expecting her to roll her eyes at Daniel's corny pun.

Instead, she gave a genuine laugh. "That's cute."

Was she for real? I tried to catch Elle's eye so we could swap *What parallel universe have we entered into?* looks, but Brandon's sudden "Ew!" averted my attention.

"Dude, what's *in* this?" Brandon grimaced at his Heavenly Hazelnut. "It tastes sludgy."

Daniel took a sip from Brandon's outstretched cup. "I must've put soy milk in. Sorry."

I glanced at Daniel worriedly, wondering if he was coming down with something.

And then I got my second shock of the day.

"Nadine?" a familiar voice said, and I turned to find my father standing behind me.

"Dad?" I was rattled. My dad hadn't set foot in the Snug Mug since my mom had left. Marley had once told me that Mom used to come here all the time, armed with travel guides to plan trips she and my dad would never actually take. I couldn't blame my dad for not wanting to come back. In fact, he looked pained to be here now, his face drawn, his lips pressed together. "What's wrong?" I asked.

"Nothing's wrong." But he squirmed, fiddling with the zipper of his vest. "I need to talk to you about something." He brushed a hand through his graying hair. "At home."

My pulse quickened. "Um, sure. Okay." Daniel gave me a questioning look, but I could only shrug. I didn't have any idea what this was about.

"I'll see you guys later." I grabbed my cello, offering my friends an uncertain wave as I followed Dad out the door.

I sat at the kitchen table as Dad ladled Crock-Pot chili into two bowls. The quiet of our two-bedroom cottage was a heavy and sustained caesura around us.

Dad was sort of like a rabbit, sometimes poking his head out of his warren, but retreating if he sensed the smallest shift in the wind. He took me to the doctor when I was sick, and made sure he kept the kitchen stocked with my favorite snacks for packed lunches. When he noticed how much I loved classical music, he'd rented me a used cello and gotten me private lessons with Maestro Claudio. He cared about me. He just didn't say it aloud.

More often than not, Daniel came over to our house for dinner. I'd started asking him over because he livened things up with his jokes and laughter. After we ate, we'd do our homework together. Daniel's mom worked long hours as an ER doctor at the hospital in Rutland. Since Daniel's dad had died, his mom couldn't handle being home too much, so she escaped into her job. She had the same look of vacant loneliness that my dad did. Maybe that was why Daniel and I had become best friends years ago. We were two only-child magnets clinging to each other for the company we couldn't find in our own families.

But Daniel wasn't here right now, and, as Dad sat down facing me, I wished he were. Dad didn't look like he was enjoying our current awkward silence any more than I was, and spent an inordinate amount of time fishing around in the box of oyster crackers.

"Isn't it a little early for dinner?" I asked, attempting to start the conversation.

"Is it?" Dad remarked absently as he sprinkled crackers into his bowl.

"It's only four thirty." I gave a small laugh that ricocheted around the kitchen.

"Oh. Right." He scratched at the back of his neck. "Sorry. I've been distracted."

I took two half-hearted bites of the chili, and then I couldn't wait anymore. "What's going on, Dad?"

He stared into his bowl. "It's about your mom." He met my eyes tentatively, then looked toward the front door, probably mapping out an escape route.

My heart dropped. "Is she okay?" A small voice inside my head said that I shouldn't care, since I hadn't *seen* her for six years and hadn't heard from her in months.

Mom had found her grand adventures and sidewalk cafés, but she'd done it half a world away from us. Occasionally, she'd send emails from remote corners of the planet. "You'll never guess where I am," they usually started, with a "You must be so big by now!" thrown in for good measure. Then there were the souvenirs that arrived in the mail sporadically, from places I'd never even heard of, like Tristan da Cunha or the Siwa Oasis. She never stayed in any one place for long, and some spots she traveled to were so remote that she couldn't stay in touch easily (or so she said). I made a conscious effort *not* to think about my mom often, as a matter of self-preservation.

"She's fine," Dad said. "In fact," he continued with forced brightness, "she's moving back to the States. Just outside of Boston."

"Really?" I tried to make it sound offhanded, like it didn't matter where she lived, since she'd backpacked herself out of my life anyway. "Why?"

Dad swirled his spoon around his chili. "She's gotten a full-time job, working with refugees at Save the Children."

"That's cool," I said quietly, meaning it. Mom was always volunteering wherever she trekked to, working with aid organizations to build houses or dispense food and clean water.

Working with refugees sounded right up her alley. "Is that what you wanted to tell me?"

Dad hesitated. "She's asked if . . ." His voice faltered. "She's asked to see you."

"What?" My spoon clattered into the bowl. My throat burned with a rising anger. "Are you kidding? After all this time?"

Dad rubbed his forehead. "I'm as surprised as you are. When you were smaller, I hoped she would try to . . ." He cleared his throat, then tried again. "She was barely twenty when we had you. She hadn't seen anything of the world yet, and—"

"I know." I rolled my eyes. "She had an irresistible wanderlust." I stood up to dump my uneaten chili into a Tupperware container for later. "You've been making the same excuse for her since I was in second grade!" I spun to face him. "You were as young as she was. And *you* didn't leave!"

Dad sighed. He worried his napkin, rolling and unrolling its edges, and I could tell he wanted to dive back into the safety of his warren. He stood and stuck his chili in the fridge. "I'm going to the lab for a while."

Dad was an arborist who specialized in rare tree diseases. He worked at one of the University of Vermont's satellite offices, studying Woodburn's elm trees. But he hardly ever went back to the lab after I got home from school. He was using the lab as an excuse to escape, but I didn't call him on it. I was ready to drop the subject, too. But Dad paused at the front door, his expression so wretched that my heart panged.

"Maybe consider it?" he asked, and I shook my head.

"Consider it? Did she consider *me* when she walked out?" His face sagged further, but I headed for the stairs that led to my bedroom. "I don't want to see her," I said flatly. "Not now. Not ever."

As I expected, my words were met with silence, followed by the soft click of the front door shutting. I paused on the stairs, my heated resolve dissolving into confusion. Taking out my phone, I typed Code Red and let the text fly. Daniel and I had used the term ever since we were little. It meant, "Drop everything and *run*—do not walk—to your BFF no matter the hour or place." Neither one of us had ever ignored a "Code Red," and

I knew Daniel wouldn't now. So I sank onto the bottom step, waiting for his reply.

An hour later, I hurried back into the Snug Mug with my cello in tow. The afternoon's crowd of after-schoolers and leaf peepers had been replaced by the more serious coffee shop set—the aspiring writers, grad students, and angsty artists. Sometimes, the shop held poetry readings or spontaneous acoustic guitar performances. Tonight, though, the shop was filled with the quieter hum of low conversations accompanied by the welcome fizzing of the espresso machine's milk steamers.

I glanced behind the counter, but Daniel was nowhere to be seen. Marley caught my eye over the top of the espresso machine, then nodded toward the loft. "He's upstairs."

I thanked him and climbed the stairs to find Daniel sitting on the loft's threadbare couch, waiting for me. The loft served as Marley's office, but aside from the haphazard mounds of receipts and files piled in one corner, it wasn't much of an office at all. More often than not, Marley could be found napping in the corner hammock as he listened to the Doors on his vintage turntable. Shredder liked to nap on the couch, and Daniel and the other Snug Mug employees used it as a makeshift break room. The loft was where Daniel and I had learned to appreciate the priceless crackle of old vinyl records and also where we went whenever we needed to talk away from the café chaos downstairs.

Daniel jumped up, and relief washed over me when I saw that his strange Kiya-induced delirium was gone.

"God, Nadi," he said, opening his arms. "This is *some* Code Red."

I sank into his hug, grateful. Daniel's hugs were always enveloping, showing how much he cared. They were one of his many awesome BFF qualities.

"I have reinforcements." He motioned toward the rickety coffee table; there was a plate with a waffle on it, plus a mug of Pumpkin Spice Supreme, both heaped with clouds of whipped cream. The waffle was also topped with Teddy Grahams, toasted marshmallows, and chocolate syrup.

Even though I was still reeling from my dad's news, an

involuntary smile spread across my face at the sight of the waffle. "Is that what I think it is?"

"Nadine's Song." He propped my cello in the corner and set the waffle plate in my hands. "It got us through the first Code Red, didn't it? So I figured . . ."

"Thank you." I plopped down on the couch and took a grateful, heaping bite, relishing the crispy, caramel sweetness of the waffle combined with the gooey, warm chocolate and whipped cream. The memory of the first time I tasted this waffle came back to me. It was on the night after Mom left. I'd had enough of putting on a brave face for my dad, who'd been trying (and failing) to act like everything would be fine. So, I'd retreated to my bedroom with my cello.

Soon, my by-the-book practicing turned into my discovery of a new, mysterious melody on the strings. I got lost in the song I was composing, and that was when seven-year-old Daniel wandered into my bedroom with a thermos and a plate full of misshapen, undercooked waffles.

"Omma is downstairs talking to your dad," he'd said, using,

like he always did, the Korean word for "Mom." I'd quickly put away my cello, embarrassed that he'd heard me playing a nonsense song. "She says I better not say anything to make you cry."

"I'm not going to cry," I told him stubbornly. Even though I'd been secretly crying on and off in my bathroom all day, I didn't want to admit it.

He scooted onto the bed beside me, and our feet, which couldn't yet reach the ground, started swinging in unison. "That was a pretty song you were playing. What was it?"

I shrugged. "I made it up."

"You're a composer." He nodded appreciatively. "Cool."

He said *composer* so matter-of-factly. And the moment he said it, the truth of it solidified inside me, a pearl of purpose that made the awfulness of what had just happened a little more bearable. *A composer*, I thought, *that's what I am*. And from that day forward, I was.

"I brought some hot chocolate," Daniel had said then, holding up the thermos. "And Omma cooked a batch of *samgyetang* for you and your dad. It's her special Korean ginseng chicken soup. It's good, but

I thought you might like these better." He set the plate of waffles in my lap. "According to my mom, waffles were the only thing I wanted to eat after my dad . . ." He glanced down at his feet, which stopped swinging. "I thought they might help." He pointed to the Teddy Grahams and marshmallows atop the waffles. "I added stuff to make it extra sweet . . ." He smiled. "Like you."

"Thanks." I took a bite. "It's really good."

"It can be your special waffle." He thought for a second, then glanced at my cello. "We can call it Nadine's Song?"

I laughed. "Sounds pretty fancy for a waffle."

"It's perfect." He nudged my shoulder. "We're both missing parents now. They're just gone to different places." We sat with that for a minute, and then he added, "It's going to be okay."

I blinked back tears. "How do you know?"

"Because we have each other," he'd said. And he'd been right.

Everything *had* been okay, relatively speaking, until tonight. Now I opened my eyes to find Daniel dipping a fork into the other side of my waffle, and I playfully tried to shove his hand away. But of course, I let him swipe a huge bite.

"So," he said as we both dug in. "Tell me the whole story."

He listened intently as I vented about the many, *many* reasons why it was completely unfair of my parents to railroad me with this.

"Especially right now," I finished. "Don't they get how huge this Interlochen audition is for me? I can't afford distractions. But I have to deal with being guilted into seeing my mom!"

Daniel stared at the smear of whipped cream swirled on the now-empty plate. "I'm not sure they're guilting you into it," he said quietly. "They're testing the waters."

I balked. "It's total manipulation!" I drained the last of my latte in one furious gulp, which made Daniel laugh.

"Maybe I should've made that decaf," he joked, but then his expression turned serious. "Nadi, you have every reason and right to be angry, but I wonder . . ." He ran a hand through his dark brown hair, making a few waves fall into his eyes. "I just think about my dad sometimes, and how I would give anything to have had more time with him."

My heart squeezed at the mention of his dad. "I know," I said softly, "but your dad didn't make a choice to leave. My mom did. Your dad loved you, and my mom . . ." My voice cracked as hurt rose inside me. "I've made up my mind." I straightened my shoulders. "Let's not talk about it anymore, okay?"

Daniel seemed on the verge of saying more, but he nodded. He stood up and retrieved my worn cello case. "So . . . am I going to hear your tour de force or what?"

"I thought you'd forgotten about it," I said, already sliding out my cello and bow. My rented cello was as tired-looking as its case, and it bore the scars from its prior players' misuse. I dreamed of having my own cello someday, and I saved as much babysitting money as I could, but it would be a long, *long* time before I could afford one. Now I brushed a hand over the weary cello, wishing I could coax it into giving me the rich tone I wanted to hear whenever I played. Then I looked at Daniel. "You know, you were sort of spacey earlier today."

"Oh, Marley's news threw me, that's all." His tone was casual, but even in the loft's dim light, I saw his blush. He motioned to my cello. "Let's hear it, maestro."

I thought about bringing up Kiya, and how entranced he'd seemed by her. But why should I when Daniel said it was no big deal? Besides, I was finally getting the chance to play for him, and I'd been waiting for it all day.

"Here goes." I sat down in Marley's straight-backed office chair and raised the bow to the strings. My piece was a prelude with slow-moving slurs. As I played, my eyes closed, and then the magical moment happened—the moment that had made me fall in love with the cello in the first place. The music moved from the cello and through me, until we were both filled with never-ending notes.

As I played the final note and lifted my bow from the cello's neck, the world gradually rematerialized around me.

Daniel was staring at me, wide-eyed.

I shifted self-consciously. "Was it awful?"

He didn't have a chance to answer before clapping and whistling erupted from the customers downstairs. "Encore!" Marley's voice shouted up to me.

I blushed and tucked my head against my cello's neck. "Omigod, everyone was listening."

"It would've been hard not to." Daniel smiled. "That piece was phenomenal." He leaned toward me, his eyes bright with pride. "You are going to be the next Interlochen summer camp prodigy. You'll see."

"I hope so," I whispered, my stomach tightening with nerves.

Just then, our phones buzzed simultaneously.

Daniel got to his first. "It's Omma, telling me to come home."

I held up my screen. "Dad. Saying the same thing." We both laughed.

I quickly packed up my cello and, within minutes, Daniel and I were standing at the street corner where we always parted ways. The mountains hugging our valley made the darkness of the night even deeper, but the bright moon and spray of stars overhead steeped the street in a milky purple glow. I tucked my chin into my jacket collar as the chilly air nipped my cheeks.

"Call me later if you need to talk more," Daniel said as I turned in the direction of my house. I responded with one last wave.

I was smiling when I reached our house, but felt some of my renewed good mood slip away as I saw our empty family room, and Dad's already-shut bedroom door. This was not a house of chaotic family chatter or rowdy board game nights. This was a lonely house.

But this summer, I'd get my chance to be at Interlochen, with my music and an entire dormitory full of laughter and chaos to keep me company. Nothing—not family drama, and certainly not a mom who hadn't been a true mom in years—was going to distract me from my goal.

Chapter Three

"Nadi, come on! Get up! I need your help."

Bright and early the next morning, I dragged my eyes open. Daniel was standing at the foot of my bed with a very large, very full garbage bag. He looked wide awake and way too cheerful for . . . What time was it, anyway? I glanced at my phone and nearly tossed it at Daniel's head.

"It's five thirty in the morning!" I cried, glaring at him.

Daniel grinned. "Isn't it great?"

Just then, Dad's head appeared above the top step of the stairs leading to my loft. He had always been an early riser, but even *he* was yawning. He gave me a sheepish shrug as way of apology. "He was very persistent" was all Dad said before going back downstairs.

Years ago, my dad had gotten used to Daniel's frequent presence in our house and also to the odd hours of his comings and goings. My loft bedroom, opening as it did onto the family room below, made it easy for Dad to keep an eye on us. Dad also knew that Daniel had been through the ringer with his dad's death and that Daniel's mom wasn't home much.

"It's got to be tough on him," Dad had remarked once. "That's one sad house he lives in."

How ironic, I'd thought then, that Dad could see that about Daniel's house but not ours.

Now Daniel held out a to-go coffee cup. "I didn't have any pumpkin puree at home, so I made you something new. I call it . . ." He fanned out a hand as if he were a magician unveiling a fantastic trick. "The Gingerbread Giant."

"*Daniiiiel.*" I groaned. "What are you doing here?" But I already knew. This had happened before. Whenever Dan showed up at our house at an ungodly hour of the morning or night, it was because he'd concocted one of his grandiose "go big or go home" plans. Daniel had the kindest heart of anyone I knew, and there was no limit to what he would do to help people or to cheer them up. When I'd had my tonsils removed, he'd filled our mailbox with twenty confetti party poppers to welcome me home from the hospital (yes, all of them popped at the same time). There were countless other surprises he'd sprung on me and my friends, and they were admittedly awesome. However, they could also be exhausting (exhibit A: the five a.m. wake-up call).

Now, as if on cue, Daniel said, "So last night after I said goodbye to you, I had this amazing idea."

Surprise, surprise, I thought dryly, taking a long, much-needed swig of the coffee he'd practically shoved into my hands. The ginger zinged pleasantly over my tongue, and so did some other ingredients I couldn't quite put my finger on. "Mmm." I nodded appreciatively. "It's not just ginger, it's—"

"Honey and orange zest." Daniel looked very pleased with himself. "Oh, and a dash of turmeric."

"It's good, but *not*"—I held up my finger—"my Pumpkin Spice Supreme."

He rolled his eyes. "You are such a creature of habit."

"Yes, and you're messing with my morning routine." I yawned and got out of bed, heading for the bathroom. "What's this amazing idea?" I called from next door.

"I was thinking . . ." I heard Daniel say. "How great it would be to make Kiya feel welcome on her first day of school?"

I froze, my toothbrush halfway to my mouth. "Kiya?"

"Yeah. She's switching schools, and she doesn't know anyone here. So I swung by the grocery store last night and got this . . ."

I flung open the bathroom door, only to be met by a multicolored helium balloon that read WELCOME!

I yelped in surprise, then pushed past it into my room. "Where did that come from?"

He laughed. "I had it in the garbage bag. I didn't want to spring it on you when you were half asleep."

"Correction. I'm *still* half asleep," I groused. Daniel had only just met Kiya, and already he'd planned an elaborate surprise for her? This was even more over the top than usual for him.

Daniel wasn't fazed by my tone and kept grinning like the balloon was the best idea since the invention of chocolate. "I need your help, Nadi. I don't want her to know this was my idea. That would be ruining the fun. Besides, you're at school early most mornings anyway, so if the security guards see you, it won't seem out of the ordinary that you're there."

This was true. I often went to school early for chamber orchestra rehearsals or Maestro Claudio's lessons, and I pretty much had a free pass to use the music room for extra practice sessions. Maestro Claudio knew I was applying to Interlochen and wanted me to use the room because of its good acoustics.

"And," Daniel continued, "your locker is right by Kiya's. She told me her locker number yesterday when she was at the Snug Mug." He tucked the balloon back into the garbage bag. "Just tie the balloon to her locker vent. That's it!"

I didn't have any valid reason for saying no to Daniel, and yet I felt a low-grade and unfounded irritation at this entire plan.

But shouldn't I *want* Kiya to feel welcome at our school? And wasn't this a nice way to do that?

Finally, I sighed and nodded. "Okay. I'm in."

"Great! But we've got to get to school now, before everybody else shows up."

I sent Daniel downstairs so I could get changed, rolling my eyes the whole time.

The school was quiet as Daniel and I walked into the building.

"If anybody asks what you're doing in the hallways," Daniel whispered, "tell them you forgot your cello bow in your locker."

"And I happened to be lugging around an enormous balloon, just for fun?" I shook my head. "And what excuse do *you* have?"

He grinned. "Hey, when you have my charm, you don't need excuses."

I couldn't help laughing. It always amazed me how Daniel could fly by the seat of his pants without stress, especially since stressed was *my* constant state of being.

"Where are you going?" I asked as Daniel headed down the hallway in the other direction.

"To the equipment room to hang with Liam and Graham until the bell rings." The equipment room housed the school's intercom system and was where our classmates Graham and Liam made the morning announcements each day. "I'm incognito, remember?" And with that, he was gone.

I walked down the hallway, past flyers about the upcoming Fall Formal, and found Kiya's locker a few down from my own.

I finished tying the balloon to Kiya's locker vent just as the first students swarmed the hallway for the day. Quickly, I slipped into the girls' bathroom before anyone might guess I was the balloon deliverer.

Mission accomplished, I texted Daniel. See you at lunch.

You rock, he wrote back. Can't wait to hear how she reacts. I want a full report.

I sighed. Of course he did. He loved hearing how his surprises went over.

As I swung open the bathroom door, I spotted Kiya walking down the hallway, studying a slip of paper in her hand that I guessed was her new schedule. When she reached her locker, she smiled, delighted by the balloon. Yup, Daniel had done it again. I'd played my part, and now I was relieved it was over.

A minute later, I sank into my desk in Ms. Bronski's homeroom and pulled out my music composition notebook. I wanted to spend the few minutes I had left before the bell rang getting lost in arpeggios and eighth notes. But I hadn't even written a single new note in my audition piece when someone sat down at the desk beside me with an exuberant, "Hey!"

I glanced up to see Kiya.

"Nadine, right?" She smiled brightly while the other students shuffled in and took their seats. "I'm so glad you're in my home-room. I didn't think I'd know anyone!"

I smiled and nodded, and then she leaned over my desk, peering at my notebook.

"Oh wow, Daniel mentioned that you were an amazing cellist, but he didn't say you composed, too. How cool!"

"Thanks." I warily rested one forearm across my notebook's pages, feeling as if she were sneaking a peek at my diary.

"Can I see what you're working on? I read music . . ."

"Um . . ." Suddenly I had the urge to snap my notebook shut. Composing was a very private process for me. Daniel was the only one who saw my pieces before I was ready to perform them. "It's kind of—"

The bell interrupted me, and, with relief, I was only able to offer Kiya an apologetic shrug before sliding my notebook back into my bag. Ms. Bronski began the morning announcements, and then introduced Kiya to the class.

"Kiya," she said, "tell us a little bit about yourself."

I expected Kiya to do what almost every other kid might've

done when faced with a roomful of strangers at a new school—mumble something barely audible and then stare at the floor hoping that would be the end of her suffering. Instead, Kiya strode to the front of the room exuding confidence.

"Hi, everyone. I'm looking forward to getting to know all of you." She gazed around, her eyes sparkling. "I feel welcome here already. If anyone knows who left the surprise at my locker, please thank them for me."

Normally during intros like this, kids whispered or shuffled papers, not paying any attention to a word the new kid said. Today, though, the entire room seemed spellbound.

"I grew up in New York City," Kiya went on. "I'm a third-generation Cameroonian American. My dad's parents came to America from Cameroon thirty years ago, and I can make a mean *ndolé*. Oh, and for those of you who don't know yet," Kiya added, "my family just bought the Snug Mug. My dad used to work at an investment firm in Manhattan, but my parents wanted a more relaxed lifestyle, so we came here!" She clapped her hands together, as if Woodburn were the best place in the world to live. "I love theater, and started acting in off-Broadway plays when I was five. I also love volunteering, and worked at my mom's nonprofit theater with her troupe of actors with special needs. And . . . well, that's all for now."

Kiya gave another dazzling smile and took a step in the direction of her desk, but a dozen hands shot up around the room.

"What plays did you perform in?" Georgette blurted, while Ben called out, "Have you ever been on TV?"

Kiya answered enthusiastically as everyone hung on to her every word. More questions came, and more, until Ms. Bronski finally put an end to them to hand out some classwork.

When the bell rang, Kiya stepped out into the hallway surrounded by a circle of kids, including Georgette, one of the school's most popular girls. Everyone was inviting her to sit with them at lunch all at once.

I didn't expect her to give me a second glance as she walked away with her new groupies, but she glanced over her shoulder to offer me a cheery, "See you later, Nadine!"

I waved back with the unsettling sensation that a momentous

shift in our school's social hierarchy was occurring. As Kiya disappeared down the hallway, I had the hunch I was watching the next Woodburn Middle School queen bee rise to her throne.

"So?" Daniel plunked his lunch tray down beside mine and scooched in between me and Elle at our table in the cafeteria. "Were you there when Kiya got to her locker? How did she react?"

"I'm glad to see you, too, Daniel," I kidded. "And I've had a wonderful morning of math pop quizzes and social studies documentaries, thanks for asking."

Daniel flicked a carrot in my direction, but I deftly dodged it. "Okay, okay." I laughed. "Kiya was thrilled about the balloon. In homeroom, she said that if anyone knew who orchestrated the surprise, to be sure to thank them for her."

"Yes!" Daniel pumped his arm in victory, then dug into his turkey wrap. "I can't believe you have homeroom with her. You're so lucky."

"Why?" The word came out harder than I'd intended.

Daniel shrugged and leaned forward, his hair falling into his face, but not before I caught the blush sweeping his cheeks. "She seems cool. That's all."

"That's all?" Elle eyed him and exchanged a look with me. "You've never paid this much attention to a new student before."

"Well, you definitely don't need to worry about Kiya making friends." I nodded toward Kiya, who was sitting a few tables over, surrounded by Georgette and a dozen other kids.

"She'll be a legend before the day's out," Elle added as Brandon sat down beside her. "In science class, I heard that she and her parents spent last summer in Peru building houses for Habitat for Humanity."

"Oh, I can top that," Brandon said. "Somebody told *me* that, back in the city, Kiya's family had Lin-Manuel Miranda over to their house for dinner. *And* that he gave them front-row tickets to *Hamilton*."

"So, they're the perfect family?" I scoffed. "Come on." All three of my friends turned to stare at me, and now *I* was the one who was blushing. "Doesn't it sound . . . too good to be true?"

"Don't be such a skeptic, Nadi," Daniel said with rare seriousness. "I'm no expert, but her family sounds awesome to me."

There was a longing in his tone that made me wince. Of course, in comparison to Daniel's home life—or, for that matter, mine—Kiya's did seem pretty perfect.

I glanced in Kiya's direction, her eyes caught mine, and she waved at all of us.

Daniel instantly stood with his tray. "I'm going to say hi. Anybody else want to come?"

I glanced at Brandon and Elle, but they were busy feeding each other grapes.

"I'm still eating . . ." I let my voice die away, hoping he wouldn't push me to come.

He didn't.

Instead, he nodded. "See you at the Mug later. I've got to get there on time for once. I promised Kiya that I'd show her the ropes. And I have to help get supplies ready for the shop's Fallfest booth. No rest for the weary." He stuck out his chest in a theatrical boasting pose that elicited eye rolls from all three of us.

I smiled at his antics, but as he walked away, I had the sinking feeling that he wasn't leaving our table, but leaving *us*. It wasn't logical, but that didn't matter. I didn't like it, and I didn't want it to happen for real. Ever.

Chapter Four

After school, Elle and I walked down Main Street, past business owners decorating their storefronts and lawns with leaf garlands, pumpkins, scarecrows, and hay bales for Sunday's festival. Each year, there was a town-wide competition for who could build the best hay bale "art" display, and already there was an impressive hay bale dragon rising up in the Sandersons' yard.

"This year's competition is going to be fierce," I said.

Elle nodded. "Brandon says the Blaze is going to be more impressive than ever, too."

In two days, the festival's booths and food tents would line this street, all leading people toward the base of Killington Peak, where there'd be hayrides, a corn maze, and the grand opening of this year's Big Pumpkin Blaze. Even now, along the mountain's base, a field of orange pumpkins glowed in the afternoon light. Beckoning tourists and townsfolk alike, those jack-o'-lanterns would be stacked into elaborate shapes and designs, maybe even into a pumpkin Empire State Building or hippopotamus. Who knew? Every year's Blaze was different. But starting at sunset on Sunday, those thousands and thousands of pumpkins would be blazing every night for two months straight, giving our valley a nightly beautiful, autumnal glow. It made me smile just to think about it, and put me more in the mood for my Pumpkin Spice Supreme than ever.

When I walked into the Snug Mug, though, Daniel didn't even glance in my direction.

He and Kiya were standing in front of the espresso machine, their foreheads nearly touching. The two of them were deep in conversation as Daniel put his hand over Kiya's to help her lock the espresso portafilter into the machine.

"Looks like somebody's got a protégé," Elle mumbled.

I nodded as we squeezed into the papasan chair together. I stared at Daniel and Kiya while they worked. When Kiya shook the whipped cream dispenser and accidentally sprayed white spritz all over herself, she squealed.

"Omigod!" She laughed, brushing the cream from her apron. "I'm completely hopeless."

"You'd think she's never made coffee before in her life," I muttered.

Then Kiya waved at us. "Nadine! Elle! Your drinks are coming right up!"

Elle smiled at her. When my own smile didn't come as quickly, Elle settled her gaze on me. "Nadi, if Daniel wants to bring Kiya into our circle, you'll give her a chance, right?" she murmured.

My stomach dipped. "What do you mean? What does Daniel have to do with this?"

Elle broke eye contact with me. "Never mind."

Kiya appeared before us, a tray of steaming coffee mugs in her hands.

"Your Pumpkin Spice Supreme." Kiya proudly placed my cup on the coffee table. "And your Raspberry Mocha," she added to Elle. She tucked the tray under her arm, and then smiled at us expectantly. "Would you mind tasting them? I want to make sure I got them right."

"*You* made these?" I blurted in surprise.

"I want to learn all the Snug Mug ins and outs, and Daniel said you'd go easy on me, so . . ." She twirled one of her curls around her finger, looking eager to please.

Elle sipped hers. "Mmm. It's delish. Thanks."

"Yay!" Kiya gave a mini clap, then glanced at me, waiting.

I picked up the mug—*my* special YOU HAD ME AT CELLO mug, which had never been used to make my Pumpkin Spice Supreme by anyone other than Daniel. For a split second, I wished that something would be wrong with the drink, so that I could point it out to Kiya. When I took a sip, though, I tasted perfection. In fact, if Kiya hadn't admitted it, I never would've known the difference between her coffee and Daniel's.

"It's great," I said quickly just as Daniel came over.

"I'm so relieved," Kiya said.

"I told you they'd love them," he said to her. "We'll tackle chai lattes next."

I waited for him to plop down in the nearby beanbag to hang out for a bit. But he just kept beaming at Kiya.

The spell was only broken when Kiya noticed her dad coming down the stairs from the loft. "Look what I made, Dad." She proudly pointed out our drinks.

"Great job, hon," he said absently as he thumbed through a pile of papers in his hand. "I've got to ask Marley about these inventory lists." He scanned the shop until he spotted Marley at the cash register. "And about cleaning out that loft space ASAP."

"Why's he cleaning the loft?" I asked Kiya as Mr. Renaud headed in Marley's direction.

"He's planning to put café tables upstairs so we have more room for customers." Kiya glanced over her shoulder toward the sales counter. "I better go help with orders." She smiled at us. "Thanks for being my guinea pigs. See you later!"

I watched her go, then turned to Daniel, my heart hammering.

"They can't put tables in the loft! That's our—" *Hangout* was what I wanted to say, but didn't. Instead, I tried to swallow down the uncomfortable lump in my throat.

Dan looked at me with that one-of-a-kind Daniel expression that made me feel like he totally got me. "Don't worry," he whispered, "we'll find a new spot for Code Reds."

But the relief I hoped to feel at his words didn't come.

"I'm going home." I stood suddenly, and Elle and Daniel both looked surprised.

"Everything okay?" Daniel asked.

I shouldered my bag. "I want to do some work on my audition pieces, that's all." I smiled a goodbye, but it felt tight and unnatural.

As soon as I was outside, the smile slipped from my face. I liked my life orderly and predictable. But now there was talk of renovating the Snug Mug, and for the first time ever, Daniel hadn't been the one to make me my drink. All I wanted to do right now was go home and feel my cello's strings under my fingertips. My bow singing across the strings, my music resonating from deep inside my cello's heart—those were certain and unchangeable. They were what I needed right now.

A crisp breeze was blowing as I reached our porch, and my mood lifted at the sight of the dancing leaves. I loved playing my cello in front of our large family-room window this time of year. Gazing out on the sunset-hued maple trees, I'd find rhythms in the twists and twirls of fiery leaves that I'd mimic on the cello.

For a split second before I opened the door, I imagined Dad being on the other side of it, maybe fixing something for dinner (besides our weekly chili staple). I imagined the two of us talking easily, the way I'd hear Elle talking to her mom when I was over at the Castillos' house. Elle's house was full of dropped backpacks, her brothers' ice hockey gear, and the warm scent of her mom's famous paella.

But as I walked into my own house now, all I found was a note from Dad on the entryway table, telling me he might be late tonight. He'd had to drive out to Burlington to meet with a professor of dendrology to discuss a problem with diseased elms.

I sighed, about to turn away from the note, when the blinking light on our landline caught my eye. We had a new voice mail. I picked up the phone to listen, and my stomach fell at the sound of an oddly-still-familiar voice from the past.

"Hi, Mike . . . and Nadi. This is Robin." It had been months since I'd actually heard my mom's voice, but I could tell by its slight waver that she was nervous. "I'm settled in my new apartment, and I wanted to give you my home number. You have my cell, but . . . I want . . . I *plan* to be more reachable now." A string of numbers followed, and then a long pause. I wondered if she'd hung up. Then she added a rushed, "I hope you'll call me."

I barely registered the message ending with a soft click. I kept the phone to my ear.

I plan to be more reachable, she'd said. Was I supposed to read that as a peace offering or a veiled apology? I hardly knew, and I didn't care, either.

I took a deep breath and deleted the voice mail. I wouldn't tell Dad anything about the message. The evidence had been erased, and I could move on and forget about it, once and for all.

But an hour of belabored cello practice later, my resolve wasn't working. I'd waited in vain to find that blissful moment when I got so completely lost in the music that everything else faded away. It wasn't happening. And I wasn't moving on from Mom's message, either. I was stuck.

Sighing, I texted Daniel: Can you come over? We can watch The 100.

I thought for sure Daniel would jump at my offer. *The 100* was his current dystopian-TV obsession. But when his response finally came, I frowned at my screen.

Can't tonight. Staying late at work to help Kiya. Rain check?

I slumped back in my chair, stunned. I couldn't remember Daniel ever saying no to our hang time before. I picked up my cello with newfound zeal. Fine, then. If Daniel was too busy to come over, I was too busy to have him over. I poised my bow over the cello, and then swooped down on the strings violently, ripping into Rimsky-Korsakov's "Flight of the Bumblebee" with a vengeance. My left hand flew up and down the cello's neck while my right drew the bow across the strings in a frantic seesaw.

Soon my fingers and arms burned, but I didn't quit. I ripped through a dozen of the fastest pieces I knew, and then worked on my audition piece, picking it apart to perfect it, measure by measure.

I had goals. I knew what I wanted and that my cello was my golden ticket. I wouldn't think about Daniel or my mom. I wouldn't think about anything else.

I woke to the jarring vibration of my phone on the pillow beside my head. I reached for it without opening my eyes, planning to turn it off. Today was Saturday, I remembered groggily, and I'd practiced until after midnight. Dad had come home around nine to find me sweating through my third hour of playing, but he knew better than to try to convince me to quit. When I binge-practiced, nothing could stop me. Now, though, I was entitled to a decent sleep-in.

But as I glanced at my phone, I saw a text from Daniel. He had new coffee ideas for tomorrow's Fallfest, and he wanted me to meet him at the Snug Mug for taste testing. I had to laugh.

Maybe this could be a chance for us to have one-on-one time, to fix whatever weirdness had suddenly cropped up between us.

I texted him back, and pulled on my favorite yoga pants and hoodie. Five minutes later, I was on my way to the Snug Mug, the memory of yesterday's bad mood fading in the face of the crisp breeze. I was smiling to myself as I passed the Sandersons' now-finished hay bale dragon, which loomed at an impressive height and had been spray-painted green.

Suddenly I was hit squarely in the face by a handful of leaves.

"Wha—?" I exclaimed, then shrieked as Daniel leapt out from behind the dragon's tail, more leaves ready in his fists.

"Gotcha!" he cried gleefully, laughing.

Not about to let him get away with his leaf bombing, I spotted an enormous leaf pile in front of Sweetie Pie's Bakery and made a dive for it. I wasn't quick enough, though, because Daniel caught me around the middle, and then we were both falling sideways into the pile.

Leaves exploded around us as we laughed breathlessly and tried to stuff leaves into each other's jacket collars. Suddenly, we were nose to nose, the brilliant leaves a prism of color around us. My pulse thundered as we locked eyes, and my heart fluttered inexplicably.

Then, just like that, we were pulling apart, both of our faces flushed from laughter and exertion. Daniel offered me a hand to help me to my feet, but there was a minute where neither one of us knew where to look or what to say, and we both focused sheepishly on the ground. Then he cleared his throat and nudged my shoulder, grinning. "I so had you, didn't I?"

I *pshawed* and nudged him back, and then we were in sync again, razzing each other as we walked the last few steps to the Snug Mug. When we opened the shop's door, we found Marley on the other side of it, two large boxes balanced in his arms.

"I've got to take these last few boxes home." He looked at Daniel. "You okay to hold down the fort before Mr. Renaud comes to open up shop?"

"Aye, aye, cap'n," Daniel said.

As I shrugged off my coat, Daniel busied himself behind

the counter, pulling half a dozen ingredients from the cabinets. When I joined him, he cocked his head at me.

"So . . . how many hours did you practice last night, anyway?"

He knew me too well. I held up my left hand, fingers spread to show all five. "I've never been so thankful for calluses in my entire life."

He whistled low. "You haven't practiced like that since last Christmas Eve."

"You mean the Christmas Eve where my mom promised she'd call and didn't?" I bristled at the memory of watching *It's a Wonderful Life* in a purgatorial loop as I waited pointlessly by the phone.

He nodded. "That was the one. She had a good excuse, though."

"Right. I think last year's was digging a fresh water well for a village in Cambodia." My anger at Mom always came with a fresh helping of guilt on the side, because it wasn't as if she'd left me to sail around the world on a yacht, or even to start another family. She was actually helping the world, which made it doubly hard to hate her for it.

"This is exactly why I don't need her back in my life. Her promises don't mean anything." I spat the words out.

"Hey, hey," Daniel said gently. "I didn't mean to open Pandora's box. Sorry."

"No, it's me." I stared at the floor. "I wasn't going to tell you, or anybody, but . . ." I sighed. "Mom left us a voice mail. It's official. She's moved back stateside. I . . ." I shrugged, then blurted, "I freaked out and deleted the message! And I'm not telling Dad about it, either." I shot him a look. "So don't try to convince me to."

"I wasn't going to." When I raised an eyebrow, he added, "*Okay*, I was going to."

"Don't judge me, all right?" My voice was soft and pleading. "I came to terms with my mom being gone a long time ago. I don't want a whole other Mom-dram in my life."

Daniel fiddled with the lid on the container of milk, then looked at me in complete seriousness. "Nadi, maybe you should just consider the idea?"

"What?" I stared at him.

"Your mom might've changed. People do. If she wants to try again, then—"

"You don't try again after six years!" I exclaimed, beginning to pace. "There's no coming back from that big of a mistake."

"For her or for you?" His eyes were soft with sincere care, but that didn't stop my anger from flaring.

I started for the door. "I didn't come here for this. I'm going to go—"

"Nadi, whoa, hold up!" He was in front of me before I could take two steps, his hands on my shoulders. I was scowling at the floor, but he leaned down and peered into my eyes so that I had no choice but to look at him. As soon as I saw the regret in his face, my anger weakened. "I'm sorry," he said. "I won't bring it up again. Deal?"

I sighed, then nodded. "Deal." Then I glanced back at the counter. Daniel had set out a bottle of maple syrup, a bag of pecans, cinnamon, and whipped cream. "So . . . what's the Daniel special today?"

As if I were the audience on a cooking show, Daniel raised the bottle of maple syrup, sweeping his hand in front of it. "Today, folks, we'll be brewing something truly unbe-*leaf*-able . . ." I snorted and he mock-glared, then continued, "Don't go getting all *sappy* on me now—"

"That's it!" I cried. "One more awful pun, and I pull the plug on the machine." I blocked the espresso machine, but he hip-bumped me out of the way.

"Don't disturb the master at his work."

"Oh, the master, huh? We'll see about that. Bring on the coffee challenge."

He laughed, then plunked a bag of espresso beans and the bag of pecans into my arms. "First, the grinding. Put the pecans in with the beans, two parts beans to one part pecans."

I mock-saluted, then set to work at the coffee grinder while Dan warmed the syrup in the microwave. Once the beans and nuts were blended, Daniel pressed them into the portafilter, and we watched the dark amber liquid stream into the waiting mug.

"Wow." I breathed in. "It smells incredible."

He nodded. "But it's about to get even better." He spooned syrup into the mug, stirred, and then added frothy steamed milk and a beautiful mountain of whipped cream. Atop the cream, he drizzled a thin spiral of maple syrup and a dash of cinnamon and ground chai spices. "Behold, the Maple Madness Latte." He handed me the cup.

I laughed, then did my best impression of a snooty food critic, lifting the cup to waft steam toward my upturned nose. "An *eau de maple* aroma fused with nutty undertones."

Daniel patted himself on the back with the air of a world-renowned gourmet.

I held up a finger to stop him. "But how does it taste? Perhaps Master Chef Cho has taken too great a risk with this unpredictable blend of flavors?"

"Wait, what?" he balked.

I added a taunting, "Like Icarus, perhaps he has flown too close to the culinary sun—"

"That's it!" He lunged for the mug, laughing. "Give me that cup! *I'm* taking the first sip. You're not worthy—"

I held the mug out of his reach in a fit of giggles. "It's mine! All mine!"

Daniel spun me to face him. His hands were warm around my waist, his brown eyes inches from mine. My heart raced as heat flashed over me, and for the second time today, my mind blurred. What was going on? Being this close to Dan had never fazed me before. But this was different. This *felt* different. This felt like—OMG—flirting?

My face blazed at the idea, but then the shop's door flew open, bringing in a gust of frigid air. I instantly stepped back from Dan, flustered.

"Hey, guys!" Kiya said brightly, stomping her fuzzy, pom-pommed pink boots as she came in.

Daniel's eyes lit up. "Hey!" he said. "I'm so glad you made it!"

"Wait," I whispered. "You invited her?" He'd never invited anyone else to one of our culinary sessions before, and the fact that he'd invited Kiya, of all people, stung.

But Daniel nodded like it was no big deal. "Sure," he whispered back. "She was so excited about learning the ropes yesterday, I looped her in."

"Sorry I'm a little late." Kiya gave the prettiest yawn I'd ever seen.

"No problem." Dan grinned at her. "So what sort of cool NYC drinks is your dad thinking of for our Snug Mug? Tell me a few of his faves, and we'll come up with something he'll love for the menu."

"Actually," Kiya said, "my dad's simplifying the menu. He wants more of a European-style café. Classic espressos and cappuccinos."

"What do you mean?" I did *not* like the way this sounded.

"Well . . . we have to stock so many different ingredients for these specialty drinks." She motioned to the maple syrup and pecans on the counter. "That's a lot of weird ingredients for one cup of coffee."

"Not weird," I blurted. "Unique."

"Oh, sure!" Kiya smiled amiably. "That, too! Don't get me

wrong. I loved the Gingerbread Giant I had yesterday. But my dad's a purist. He believes good coffee doesn't need bells and whistles."

Good coffee? What did she think the Snug Mug's coffee was? Dirt? The reality of what she was saying struck me full force. "So . . . no more specialty drinks. At *all*?"

She smiled, as if this were good news. "No frills needed."

My stomach dropped. No more Pumpkin Spice Supreme? Daniel's coffee creations extinct forever? I glanced at him worriedly, expecting to see him crestfallen. Instead, he looked thoughtful.

He opened his mouth, surely about to tell Kiya all the reasons why a boring menu like that would *never* work here. But instead, he said, "So . . . a more sophisticated coffeehouse. Cool."

My jaw dropped. Who was this person standing before me, calmly accepting the demise of his creations?

"When?" The word rang loudly through the shop, and they glanced at me in surprise.

"What do you mean?" Kiya asked innocently.

"When is your dad taking all of Daniel's fun drinks away?" I asked.

She looked momentarily confused, and almost a little hurt by my accusatory tone.

"Nadi—" Daniel gave me an *it's no big deal* look, but I didn't buy it.

"Oh, probably not for another couple of days," Kiya answered. "He knows how obsessed people get over pumpkin spice this time of year, so he's not making any changes until after tomorrow's festival." My chest constricted even as Kiya's smile broadened. "Anyway, I'm so excited to see what the festival is all about. I've never experienced a New England fall."

"No place does fall like Woodburn," Daniel said. "You'll love it."

She picked up my cup of Maple Madness from the counter, breathing in. "Wow. That smells amazing."

"Try it," Daniel urged.

And before I could protest, she took a long, dreamy sip that made her look as if she were in a commercial for coffee.

"Mmm. Soooo good. Can I help with the next one?"

"Sure." Daniel beamed. "What should we make, milady? Your wish is my command." He bowed, and she giggled, tilting her head coyly.

Ugh. I resisted the urge to make a face.

"I love cinnamon," Kiya offered.

"Cinnamon!" Daniel beamed. "I love cinnamon, too." He said it like it was the most amazing coincidence ever.

"Um . . ." I looked back and forth between the two of them. "Pretty much everybody likes cinnamon."

Neither of them glanced my way. Daniel was already scooping up the cinnamon, milk, and coffee beans while Kiya watched eagerly. "We could do a cinnamon swirl au lait," he suggested.

"Ooh, I just had an idea, too!" Kiya exclaimed. "My mom has this amazing recipe for cinnamon rolls. I could make some, and then tomorrow, we can wedge them onto the rims of coffee cups when people buy the cinnamon drinks."

"Do you think your dad would be okay with that?" Daniel asked. "That's pretty much the opposite of coffee in its purest form."

She laughed. "It's only for a day. I think he'll understand."

The two of them began chatting about how much milk and cinnamon to use. Soon, they seemed to forget I was there entirely.

"I can show Kiya how to steam the milk," I offered, taking a step toward Daniel.

"That's okay," Daniel said. "We've got it." He glanced at me absently. "Do you want to clear some counter space for us to work?"

"Sure," I muttered. I hastily grabbed the bag of pecans, but I grabbed the wrong end, and the nuts tipped out of the bag, spilling all over the floor. I bent to pick them up, right at the exact moment Kiya did, too. Our foreheads crashed together in a painful *thunk*.

"Ow," we said at the same time. I jerked away in pain, backing into the counter.

Something tipped against me, and warm syrup slid down my wrists and hands.

"Oh no." I gasped, then reached behind me to feel the spilled bottle of maple syrup sticking to the back of my hoodie. I held up my syrup-coated hands. Daniel's eyes glinted in amusement, but to his credit, he held back a laugh.

"Oops." Kiya giggled as she rubbed the red spot on her forehead. "Who won, Nadine? You or the maple syrup?"

"Definitely the syrup," I groused. I tried in vain to wipe some of the syrup off my hoodie. It was hopeless. I glanced at Daniel. "I should go home and clean up."

"What? No!" He started to pull off his own sweatshirt. "If you're worried about the syrup on your hoodie, you can wear mine."

"That's okay. You guys finish up." My smile tightened. "Kiya can learn from a *master*."

"Ha." He smiled back, but his expression was worried. "I'll see you tomorrow at the festival, right?"

I nodded. "I wouldn't miss it."

Kiya gave me a wave, but she was already turning back toward Daniel. As I walked out the door, I heard her say to him, "Can you show me how to lock the portafilter in place again? I can't ever get it to snap into place the right way . . ."

A vision of Daniel's hands over Kiya's came to me, and I shoved my own hands into my hoodie pockets. I didn't want to think about their hands touching. I didn't want to think about the two of them brewing coffee together. I didn't want to think about Kiya with Daniel at all.

Chapter Five

"Go, Brandon! Go!" Elle screamed.

Brandon and Daniel were both leaning over an enormous metal tub, their hands tucked behind their backs, heads dunking under the water as they tried to grab ahold of an apple.

"Come *on*, Daniel!" I clapped and whistled. "You've got this!"

He and Brandon were neck and neck in the Fallfest's bobbing-for-apples competition, with Graham and Liam following close behind. Since this was a booth run by the middle school's PTA and faculty, a dozen Woodburn middle schoolers were competing. All around us, other students and their families were cheering. By my count, both Dan and Brandon had ten apples in their piles.

"Ten seconds left!" I hollered, watching the timer counting down.

Brandon lifted his drenched head from the enormous metal tub, another apple in his mouth. Before he could drop the apple onto his pile, Daniel sprang up from the tub and sprayed a stream of water right into Brandon's ear.

Brandon yelped and dropped his apple back into the tub just as Daniel dunked one last time and came up with an apple of his own. The timer buzzed, and applause erupted from the crowd as Daniel whooped victoriously.

Then, suddenly, he scooped me into an enormous hug. My breath caught, but I wasn't sure if it was from the coldness of his damp cheek, or from his sunshine-and-cinnamon scent. As he pulled away, my heart flipped at the sight of his eyes glinting adorably in the bright sunlight, electrified with energy and happiness.

"Not too shabby," I finally said when I found my breath.

"And the three-year reign of the apple-bobbing king

continues," Dan declared, while Brandon, Graham, and Liam collectively scoffed. As the guys towel-dried their hair and faces, Principal Nyugen passed out piping-hot apple ciders to everyone.

"You fight dirty," Brandon muttered to Daniel as he finished his cider. Elle patted his arm consolingly even as she shared a secret eye roll with me.

"Come on." Daniel slung an arm over Brandon's shoulder, steering him away from the apple-bobbing tub. "You can avenge yourself in the corn maze. You always find your way out of it before I do."

"Hayride first!" Elle said, taking Brandon's hand. She beckoned us to follow them toward the tractor-drawn wagon waiting at the end of Main Street. As we walked, I breathed in the scent of honey-roasted nuts combined with the aroma of flash-fried apple cider donuts.

Sunday had dawned a dazzling blue, and gold light filtered through the flaming trees. Perfect weather for the Fallfest. Stalls sponsored by Woodburn's local businesses filled Main Street, which had been blocked off as a pedestrian-only zone for the day. Twinkling white lights and pumpkins decorated most stalls, which were selling everything fall-ish, from homegrown maple syrup to fresh-baked pies to hand-knit scarves and gloves.

I must've been smiling because as Daniel fell into step beside me he said, "Glad to see you're in a such a good mood."

I shrugged, but my smile broadened. "You know I love Fallfest."

We climbed aboard the rickety wagon. Elle and Brandon sat on a hay bale seat toward the front while Dan and I settled into the two remaining spots at the back.

"I was worried about you yesterday," Dan said as the tractor pulled out of the parking lot and puttered toward the base of Killington. "When you left the Mug, you seemed out of sorts."

"Well . . . I was." I was relieved he'd picked up on my mood. I thought he'd been so distracted by Kiya that he hadn't noticed. "I'm kind of surprised you *weren't*. I mean, we found out that the Snug Mug's about to lose all its specialty drinks. Aren't you upset? And what about Marley?"

Dan shrugged. "Marley knew this was a possibility when he sold the shop. 'New ownership, new ball game,' he said. And I agree with him. Things evolve."

"But . . . they're *your* drinks." *Our drinks*, I thought but didn't say. I gazed out at the field of orange pumpkins before us, wanting to relish the sight but fighting a tightness in my chest.

"And we'll still make them. You and me." Daniel put his arm around my shoulder. "Always." Then he grabbed a handful of hay and dangled it teasingly over my head. "Now. Enough serious talk or I'm going to be forced to take drastic measures."

I leaned away from him. "Nuh-uh. You wouldn't."

Of course, it was too late. He dropped the hay over me, and I yelped a protest, grabbing a handful to toss at him. Within seconds, everyone on the wagon was engaged in a full-blown war, tossing hay everywhere.

It was only when Ms. Franklin, scowling, pulled the tractor over and ordered everybody off that the hay blizzard stopped.

"Your fault," I chided Daniel as we stepped down from the

wagon and started the trek through the pumpkin patch back to Main Street.

He blinked innocently. "Who, me? Never." He pulled another handful of hay from behind his back and tried to stick it into the collar of my shirt, but I was too quick, ducking out of his way and running smack into—

"Kiya!" Daniel blurted.

"Hey, guys." She was surrounded by a crowd of the most popular kids at our school, looking autumn chic in her purple coat and lace-up boots. She smiled in amusement as she took in our hay-covered clothes. Beside her, Georgette and the others giggled. "How was the hay ride?"

I opened my mouth to respond, but what came out was a sneeze, which elicited a whole second round of laughter.

"Great!" Daniel said. "Are you going for a ride?"

She shook her head. "Actually, I've been looking all over for you."

"You have?" Dan beamed at her. "Do you want to walk around with us? We were going to the corn maze."

"Um, Dan? Your shift started at the Snug Mug booth fifteen minutes ago?" She said it gently, but Daniel's response was an instant slap to his forehead.

"My shift!" He groaned. "I lost track of time. I'm so sorry. Is your dad mad?"

"Not mad." She laughed. "More like desperate. He has no idea how to make your drinks. I tried but botched a few. Marley was helping out but now Dad's solo . . ."

Daniel didn't wait to hear the rest. He was already jogging ahead of us, calling over his shoulder for us to come visit him at the booth later. "For the unveiling of Kiya's Spectacular Cinnamon Swirl!" he added.

"The . . . what?" I glanced at Elle and Brandon blankly, thinking I must've heard wrong.

Kiya gave a modest shrug. "That's what he's been calling the cinnamon café au lait we invented yesterday."

Georgette snorted. "He named a drink after you?"

I bristled at the thought of how special I'd always thought my Nadine's Song waffle was. Now Kiya had a coffee named for her?

Kiya was smiling, but not in a ridiculing way like Georgette was. "I think it's sweet."

Georgette glanced at Kiya in surprise, then shrugged. An awkward silence settled over us until Brandon checked the time on his phone.

"I should head over to the Blaze headquarters," he said. "I'm supposed to help Mr. Henkels with the lighting and sound checks to make sure everything's in good shape for the kickoff tonight." He gave Elle a quick peck on the cheek. "See you guys later."

As Elle waved after him, Graham and Liam walked by, headed toward the corn maze.

"If we're not back in five hours, send a search party," Liam joked to us as they passed. Graham laughed, but his eyes fell on Kiya, and he smiled openly at her.

"Omigod." Georgette latched on to Kiya's arm once Graham was out of earshot. "Did you see that smile he gave you?" Both girls giggled. "I caught him looking your way a few times during lunch Friday, too."

"Really?" Kiya's smile widened. "He *is* totally cute."

"Ooh . . ." Georgette clapped her hands. "I *love* playing matchmaker. You don't have a date for the Fall Formal yet, do you?"

"No," Kiya answered. A wave of relief washed over me when I saw Kiya's face brighten at the possibility of going to the formal with Graham. But confusion quickly followed the relief. Why did the prospect of Kiya and Graham being together suddenly make me happy?

"Great!" Georgette grabbed Kiya's hand. "Let's catch up to them in the corn maze. He can be your knight in shining armor rescuing you from being lost in the cornstalks forever."

"Oh, come on. I don't need rescuing." Kiya rolled her eyes, but she was laughing.

Georgette was already leading her away, but Kiya looked back at Elle and me.

"Want to come along?" she asked us.

Elle nodded but I cut her off with a quick, "I haven't had my daily pumpkin spice yet. I need to be caffeinated first."

A fleeting look of—what?—crossed Kiya's face. Was it hurt?

Disappointment? It passed too quickly to tell. "See you later," she said, and then she was gone, disappearing amid the cornstalks with Georgette.

I could feel Elle's eyes on me, questioning, but I started in the direction of the Snug Mug booth, avoiding her gaze.

"You need to be caffeinated first?" Elle finally repeated as we walked. "Really, Nadi? You *love* the corn maze. What's going on?"

"Nothing," I mumbled. "I bet Kiya doesn't even like corn mazes. Or pumpkin patches. I bet it's all a ruse."

"That's a big assumption to make about someone you don't know," Elle said.

Sometimes I wished that Elle didn't always call things like they were. "Can't you let me get away with a snap judgment even *once*?" She laughed, shaking her head. I sighed. "O-*kay*. Fine. I don't get why everyone loves Kiya so much, right from the get-go."

Elle glanced at me in surprise. "Nadi, everybody's just curious about her because she's new. You know how it works. And you're the last person I'd expect to get upset about it."

"I'm not," I said stiffly. Then, as we reached the Mug's stall, I saw KIYA'S SPECTACULAR CINNAMON SWIRL written in large letters on the chalkboard menu. My stomach tightened at the sight of her name scrawled in Daniel's familiar handwriting.

But then Daniel grinned at me, and all was forgiven as he ignored the long line of customers and handed me a cup of Pumpkin Spice Supreme. "A one-of-a-kind drink for a one-of-a-kind Nadi," he said.

"You're going to get in trouble with your new boss." I nodded toward Mr. Renaud, who was looking on with an inscrutable expression. "Maybe help the customers in line first?"

"Nah," he whispered back. "You're worth breaking the rules for." Then, once he'd given Elle her Raspberry Mocha and she'd wandered away to peruse the jewelry at the adjoining booth, he added, "Hey, you want to hang out tonight after my shift is over? We could do the Blaze? There's something I've been wanting to talk to you about. And I . . . I just can't wait anymore!"

My stomach catapulted into my throat. Instantly, a vision of the two of us dancing under the twinkling lights at the Fall

Formal came into my mind. What if Daniel was going to ask me to the dance? My heart hammered at the thought, but a millisecond later, I was checking myself. Why had the dance been the first thing to pop into my mind? Daniel and I'd never wanted to go before, but . . . did I want to go now?

If I got accepted to Interlochen camp, I'd be spending this entire summer away from my lifelong friend. While the idea of camp was thrilling, the idea of leaving Daniel—even for two months—was gut-wrenching. It made me want to spend as much time with him now as possible. Going to the dance together as friends could be a nice way to cap off the year. Right?

"Cool." I smiled at him. "I don't really want to stick around for the Blaze lighting, though. We've seen it a thousand times before, and the first night is always swamped with tourists. We could watch a movie instead?"

"Perfect." He turned toward the line of customers, adding, "Gotta go."

"Me, too."

As Elle and I walked toward the corn maze, I spotted Kiya

and Graham at the pumpkin ring toss booth. They were standing close together, smitten grins on their faces. Yup, he'd be asking her to the formal in no time.

As Elle and I puzzled our way through the cornstalks, laughing at our missteps, I felt happier than I had all week. Tonight, I'd convince Daniel to talk to Mr. Renaud about keeping the specialty drinks we loved. Tonight, we'd hang out on the couch and binge on pizza, popcorn, and movies. Tonight, everything off-kilter in my life would snap back into place.

Chapter Six

"This is my favorite part," Daniel said around a mouthful of pizza, pointing to the TV, where *Ferris Bueller's Day Off* was streaming. "Wait for it . . . wait for it . . ." He laughed as, on the screen, the red Ferrari crashed through the window and landed fifty feet below. "I love it," he wheezed after he'd quit laughing.

"Nooooo, really?" I teased. "I can't tell at all!"

Daniel tossed one of the couch's pillows at me, but I blocked it with the one in my lap. We were on opposite ends of the couch, our socked feet tucked under our shared blanket. This time of year, Dad kept a fire burning in our old-fashioned potbellied stove, but our cabin was still drafty, and fleece blankets abounded to ward off the chill.

"Hey," I said as the movie ended. "Want to make s'mores after this? I have this one section of my composition I'm really struggling with, too. I could play it for you."

My words were pouring from my mouth too quickly, but I couldn't help it. Daniel and I were back in sync, laughing at the movie and pillow-fighting like the weirdness of the last three days hadn't existed at all. I was so relieved that I didn't want the night to end.

Daniel grinned, and my heart tripped. I felt like I hadn't seen that grin in ages. Or hadn't seen that grin directed at *me* in ages. The last few days, I'd only seen him smiling like that at Kiya. "You just don't want me to leave you alone with your dad," Daniel said.

"That"—I wagged a finger, about to deny it, but sighed—"is also true."

Dad had been doing fieldwork most of the day, hiking through the surrounding hills collecting bark samples from trees, which he then studied in his lab. But when he'd come home to discover Daniel and me in the midst of a movie night, he'd actually frowned. That was surprising; Dad always seemed glad to have Daniel around. When I'd gone into the kitchen for popcorn, Dad had looked up from an untouched bowl of chili to ask quietly, "How much longer will Daniel be here, do you think?"

"I don't know," I'd replied, startled. "Why?"

Dad had only shrugged and mumbled, "Never mind."

My gut told me that Dad had something he wanted to tell me. Judging from the strained look on his face, it wasn't good. And when he'd passed through the family room on his way to his bedroom while Daniel and I were mid-movie, he'd still had that strained expression.

Now Daniel was staring at me, arms crossed stubbornly. "No. I won't stay. I refuse to be a pawn in your father-daughter drama."

I cocked my head at him. "Really?"

His theatrical resolve melted into laughter. "Of course I'll stay. I told you I needed to talk to you, remember?"

My pulse quickened. *The dance.* It *had* to be about the dance.

To hide my flushing face, I walked over to the potbellied stove. I busied myself with the bag of marshmallows and roasting sticks, which I always kept at the ready in a basket by the stove.

"And I'll take your s'mores," he added, "and raise you a Crackling Campfire Cappuccino."

"A what?" I sat down before the stove, opening its hinged door and carefully balancing a marshmallow-tipped skewer over the flames.

"You'll see." Daniel smiled mysteriously, then headed for the kitchen, calling over his shoulder, "You roast the marshmallows, I'll do the rest."

Five minutes later, as I sandwiched perfectly toasted marshmallows between graham crackers and chocolate, Daniel sat down beside me on the floor. He carried a tray with two steaming, beautifully foamed cappuccinos on top. The cups were rimmed with graham cracker crumbs. Daniel slid toasted marshmallows from my skewer onto the foam in the cups, and drizzled chocolate syrup over the top. Then he handed me a cup and lifted his own.

"To new possibilities," he whispered, clinking his cup to mine.

I raised my cup to my lips and tasted the smokiness of a campfire, the richness of dark chocolate, and the sweetness of graham crackers and marshmallow blended into one satisfying sip. *Mmm.* It was *almost* as delicious as a pumpkin spice latte.

When I lowered my cup, I found Daniel gazing at me intently, his face golden from firelight.

"Nadi?" he said softly.

This is it, I thought. *He's going to ask me to the dance.* My heart was a tambourine rattling inside me as I nodded.

"Yes?"

He ran a hand through his hair, then laughed nervously. "This is going to change everything, and . . . I can't believe I'm about to say it out loud. But here goes." He sucked in a breath, then burst out with, "I like Kiya!"

The expectant smile on my face froze as shock and confusion made the room tilt around me. I braced my hands against the floorboards and stared at Daniel in disbelief. "Wh . . . what?" I finally managed.

"I like Kiya," Daniel said again, and laughed buoyantly. "I can barely believe it myself. The second I saw her, it just hit me like a lightning bolt. And now I can't stop thinking about her!" He grabbed my free hand and squeezed. "This is for real, Nadi. I'm a total goner."

I cleared my throat, my cheeks aching with a forced smile. How could this be happening? People didn't just fall in "like" in three days. I took a deep breath, knowing that how I reacted in this moment could make or break our friendship. All I could muster was an awkward, overly enthusiastic, "Wow!"

"I know, right?" Daniel laughed again. "Don't you think she's amazing?"

A million thoughts ran through my brain, but none of them had to do with Kiya being amazing. I swallowed. "Daniel, you only just met her."

"That's how these things are supposed to happen, though." Daniel's eyes shone. "The whole love-at-first-sight magic."

Love? My stomach tightened.

"I'm not sure." My words came slowly. "That didn't work out so well for my parents."

"Oh. Right." Daniel paused, frowning, then brightened with fresh optimism. "But you've said yourself that couldn't have been real. The real thing lasts forever."

I shrugged. My parents had met when they were sixteen. They'd eloped at eighteen. I had no idea what their relationship had been like. Dad never talked about it, and Mom wasn't around to ask. But "love at first sight" hadn't turned out well for, say, Romeo and Juliet, either.

Plus, there was Graham. I remembered how Kiya had seemed excited to go along with Georgette's matchmaking plot earlier today. It was probably best to tell Daniel about that before things got worse. I looked into his hopeful gaze, then dropped my own. "Daniel, what if Kiya already—"

"Has a boyfriend?" he finished. He waved a hand. "She doesn't. Not yet, anyway, so the timing is perfect."

I sighed. Even if I told Daniel about Graham, I knew my

best friend wouldn't be bothered by that. "So . . . you like her." I curled my knees into my chest. "Do you know how she feels about you?"

"I don't have a clue. But . . ." Daniel smiled. "I have a plan to win her heart." He swigged his coffee while mine grew cold on the tray. "By the time I ask her to the Fall Formal, she'll be head over heels . . ."

My stomach ached as Daniel kept talking. He'd never been thinking about asking me to the dance. All along, he'd wanted to ask Kiya. Why hadn't I guessed?

I blinked, shaking myself out of my daze to focus on what Daniel was saying.

"Of course, she won't know it's me until the end, but—"

"Daniel." I held up a hand to stop his rambling. "What are you talking about?"

"Operation Kiya." He grinned. "The dance is in two weeks. I've planned surprises for Kiya for the next five days. One surprise a day, all from her secret admirer. Then next Monday, I'll reveal that the secret admirer is me, and I'll ask her to the dance.

By then, she'll have fallen for the guy behind the gifts . . ." He stuck out his chest and pointed to himself. "Me." He smiled proudly. "See? I've got it all figured out."

I laughed a little, despite my tangle of emotions.

Daniel glanced at me, as if waiting for me to say something else. "Don't you think Kiya and I would be good together?" he finally asked. I stared at the floor for a long moment. "Nadi, don't you?"

I blew out a long breath. "Daniel, honestly? I barely know her. And neither do you." I frowned. "And I'm not so wild about her dad right now, either. He swoops into Woodburn and decides to turn the Mug into some elitist café for coffee snobs. What's that about?"

"But Kiya has nothing to do with that," Daniel said. "And sure, I'll miss making my drinks *at* the Mug, but it's only a job. I can keep making my drinks when I'm not working." He smiled and leaned toward me. "Don't worry. It'll be fine."

"It won't be the same." I shook my head. "We've always hung out at the Mug after school. And now—"

"Now what?" Daniel laughed. "Nadi, the world isn't ending. We'll hang out at the Mug regardless." He nudged my shoulder. "It'll be different, but you'll get used to it."

"No." I stood up to start cleaning up our s'mores and coffees. "I'll never get used to having Marley's Snug Mug—*our* Snug Mug—taken away. The Renauds haven't even lived in Woodburn long enough to know what sort of coffee people here want. And if I were Kiya, I wouldn't let my dad mess it up."

For the first time since he'd dropped the Kiya bomb, Daniel's smile faltered. "That's not fair. Kiya can't help what her dad does."

"Well, she could try to talk him out of it."

"Maybe she has already," Daniel suggested. "We have no idea."

"I doubt it." I swung away from him, heading toward the kitchen.

Daniel followed. "I guess I could talk to her about it. Once she falls madly in like with me, maybe she'll fight to save my endangered drinks."

I rolled my eyes. "Keep dreaming."

"Hey," Daniel said. "I dream big! You know that."

As we stood at the kitchen sink together, washing our cups and plates, Daniel asked, "So . . . will you help me with Operation Kiya?"

"Daniel . . ." I groaned. "You want me to help? Again?"

He clasped his hands and went down on one knee. *"Pleease."*

"Omigod, get off the floor." I pulled him up, both of us laughing. I wanted to say no. I wanted to tell him all the reasons why I didn't think Kiya was right for him. But I couldn't. Not when he was looking at me with those kind, hopeful eyes. I cared about him too much to disappoint him. "I'm not promising anything, but I'll see what I can do."

"Yes!" He pumped his fist, then scooped me up in a hug and spun me around. My skin tingled, my every sense on overload. A millisecond later, I stiffened in his arms, wary of my dizzying whirl of feelings. "Um, Daniel," I stammered. "Could you put me down now?"

He did, but I stumbled, and he put his hand on my waist to steady me. When I glanced up, his face was near mine. I loved the fact that he had the tiniest smear of marshmallow on the tip of his nose. That was *so* Daniel, enjoying his s'more so much that he was wearing some. I lifted my hand to wipe it off, the way I would've done any other day. But suddenly, I felt oddly self-conscious about it. I planted a flat palm on the cool counter to bring myself back to reality and said, "You've got marshmallow on your nose, you goof."

"No surprise there." He grinned and wiped it off. "So . . . I'll have the poem ready in the morning. It's going to be so great!" He pulled out his phone and began texting himself, and I could almost see the wheels of his mind spinning with love songs, red roses, and boxes of chocolate. Then he suddenly froze and looked at me. "Your composition piece!" He slapped his forehead. "You said you wanted me to listen—"

"No, it's okay." I said it with an awkward quickness that was jarring. I'd wanted to play my piece for him so badly when this evening had started, but now I wasn't in the mood. Three words were striking cymbal crashes in my brain. *Daniel likes Kiya; Daniel likes Kiya; Daniel likes Kiya.*

I faked a yawn. "I'm tired, and we have school tomorrow."

"Oh, sure. Next time, then." There was a trace of disappointment in his voice. "Can you meet me at the Snug Mug in the morning?" he asked as he grabbed his coat and headed for the door. "Operation Kiya, Day One."

I forced a nod and a wave goodbye, but my stomach sank. It sank even further when my dad walked into the kitchen, his face as pained as my heart.

"Was that Daniel leaving?" Dad collapsed, more than sat, in one of the creaky kitchen chairs.

I nodded, then, with Dad's strained face giving me a creeping feeling of dread, blurted, "I'm wiped, so I'm going to head upsta—"

"Sit." Dad rubbed his brow. "I need to talk to you."

Gulp. I knew it.

"Okay." I sat across from him. "What's up?"

"I lied to you." He met my eyes guiltily. "Earlier this week, when I told you I drove to Burlington to meet with that professor. That's not where I was." He drummed his fingertips against the tabletop, something he did when he was uncomfortable. "I went to see your mom."

"In Boston?" I asked in disbelief. Boston was almost a three-hour drive.

"We met halfway." His voice was weary. "She told me she called the house and left a message." His eyes steadied on mine, until I had to break his gaze. So . . . he'd guessed about me deleting the message, then. But all he said was, "I told her sometimes our phone is finicky."

I heaved a sigh, grateful that Dad wasn't going to make me confess. "Anyway," he went on. "I . . . I wanted to talk with her in person. About her visiting with you."

"The two of you talked about me?" My fists curled against the linoleum tabletop, my palms damp. "Without me there?"

He smiled a little sadly. "We *are* your parents. That's what parents are supposed to do."

"Yeah, well, Mom dropped the ball on that years ago," I mumbled. "You shouldn't have gone to see her without telling me."

"Maybe," he conceded, "but I thought if I went first, you might feel better about seeing her."

I stared at him. "Dad. I'll never feel better about that."

There was a long minute of silence as he stared down at the table. "She's not the same person she was when she left us." His tone was soft and regretful. "She's not a scared kid anymore, like she was back then. Like we both were, trying to raise a baby when we were ones ourselves." He slid his hand across the table toward me, but I pulled my hands into my lap. "Your mom knows you're hurt. She doesn't expect you not to be angry with her. Heck . . ." He lifted his eyes to mine. "I'm still angry with her, too."

I nearly laughed, because it seemed impossible to picture Dad angry at anyone.

"She'd just like the chance to see you," Dad continued, "only for a little while. It can end there, or you can see her again after that. We'd leave it up to you."

"No." I stood up, adamantly shaking my head. "I already told you that I didn't want to see her. I don't even know why you keep bringing it up." I started in the direction of the loft stairs, knowing Dad wouldn't follow me if I retreated to my bedroom.

"Nadine, wait." This time, Dad caught my hand, holding it in his own stiffly but steadily. "I keep bringing it up because someday, you might wish you had a relationship with your mom. You might find you need her as you get older, and I wouldn't want you to regret having passed up this chance."

I opened my mouth, about to tell him that this wasn't about what I wanted. No one was listening to what *I* wanted. But before I had the chance to get the words out, Dad pulled something from his back pocket and slipped it into my outstretched hand.

"It's a note from your mom." He gave my hand a small squeeze before letting his own hand drop. "Read the note. Think things over. That's all I'm asking."

I spun away, crushing the note in my hand as I climbed up into my loft.

An hour later, once the lights downstairs were off and I'd heard Dad's steps retreating to his bedroom, I tossed restlessly in bed, trying in vain to sleep. I'd attempted several times, over the last hour, to practice my cello, but I couldn't. My eyes were constantly drawn away from my music to the crumpled note on my nightstand. I wanted to ignore it. I wanted to burn it in the fire.

Instead, with anger and curiosity playing tug-of-war inside of me, I threw off the covers and reached for the note. Holding it up to the moonlight, I read:

Dear Nadine,

There are so many wrongs I wish I could right. There are a thousand ways I could say, "I'm sorry." None of them seem adequate or even close to what's in my heart. You might never believe my apologies or explanations, but I would still like the chance to give them. I don't expect forgiveness. I have no expectations at all. What I do have is the hope of someday seeing you, if you'll let me. Text or call anytime.

Mom

My eyes filled. I recognized her handwriting from the post-cards she'd sent me over the years. When I was younger, I used to stare at the curls and slants of her writing, trying to attach a personality to the style. Someone who looped the letter *S* the way she did was kind, I told myself. Someone who curved *Y*s in her quirky, slanted manner was funny and maybe liked to sing silly songs in the shower. The mom I knew was the one I'd made up from postcards and emails.

I slipped the note into my messenger bag and lay back on my pillow. Moms on pages were safer, I thought as I drifted off to sleep. Moms on paper could never break your heart.

Chapter Seven

"What do you think?" Daniel peered anxiously over my shoulder at the paper in my hand.

We were up in the Snug Mug's office. Below us, the shop was bustling with early birds getting their coffees before heading to work or school.

I'd hardly slept at all last night, thanks to Mom's note and Daniel's declaration of "like" for Kiya. In fact, Mom's note felt like it was burning a hole in my back pocket right this very second. But—I glanced at Daniel—at least I had a momentary distraction, even if it was a distraction that involved reading a poem written for Kiya. Sigh. I'd take what I could get.

On the upside, I had a steaming cup of pumpkin spice, and Daniel and I had a moment to ourselves.

"If you'd give me a millisecond to read it," I said to Daniel, "I'd be able to tell you." I mock-glared at him and spun away so he wouldn't hover.

"'There once was a girl from the city,'" I read aloud from the piece of paper. "'She was stylish, with eyes oh so pretty. When a lad gave her flowers, she smiled for hours, and said, 'Oh, now, isn't he witty?'"" I lowered the paper, raising an eyebrow at Daniel. "Seriously?" I asked.

Daniel watched me expectantly. "You don't like it?"

I had the urge to point out that if Kiya was anything like Elle and me, she'd rather be called smart than pretty. But I resisted. Kiya would probably roll her eyes at the cheesy poem anyway, and then Daniel's crush crusade would be finished. Part of me felt guilty for wishing that, but better he find out that Kiya wasn't right for him now than later on.

"It's fine," I said flatly, handing the paper back to him.

Daniel sighed. "Fine's not good enough. I want it to be perfect."

"Daniel . . ." There was exasperation in my tone. "I have to be at orchestra in ten minutes. It's too late to write a new poem. Just tell me what you need me to do."

He hesitated, probably debating whether or not he could pull off a Shakespearean feat in under ten minutes. Then he gave up and handed me the poem, along with a single rose. "Could you tape it to her locker with the flower?"

Just then, Daniel's phone buzzed. He glanced at the screen. "Text from Omma. She's working a double shift today. Surprise, surprise." He feigned nonchalance, but there was a hint of bitterness to his tone, and I wondered how things were in Daniel's house. He joked about how great it was to be able to stay up as late as he wanted, or eat ice cream for dinner whenever he felt like it. But almost every time I hung out at his place, his mom was working. Their fridge was a testament to takeout and frozen dinners. It made me glad that my dad's chili was as good as it was.

I couldn't help but stick a hand in my back pocket to make sure Mom's note was still there. It was, and I nearly slid it out to show Daniel, but then Mr. Renaud appeared on the steps.

"Hey, guys." He was holding a tape measure in one hand and a notepad in the other. "I need to take some measurements of the space up here. For the tables I ordered."

"Sure, Mr. Renaud. No problem," Daniel said.

"Oh, and, Daniel," Mr. Renaud said. "We're doing fifty percent off all specialty drinks until the stock is gone. The sooner we overhaul the menu, the better."

Daniel nodded. "Sounds good. I'll tell customers during my shift this afternoon."

I bristled. Why didn't Daniel care that we were losing our fave hangout spot *and* our fave drinks at the Snug Mug? Could it be that he was just going along in hopes of impressing Kiya's dad?

While Daniel grabbed our coffee cups, I texted Elle a quick emoji of a grouchy face along with the words Current Mood. I shouldered my cello case and messenger bag and made for the stairs, nearly forgetting Kiya's poem in my hurry, until Daniel called me back.

"Nadi, would *you* like the poem?" he asked in a whisper. "I mean—if I'd written it for you."

My heart tripped, and heat pricked my cheeks. "Wh-what do you mean?"

"Maybe it's too much, too fast, you know?" Daniel said. "I don't want her to think I'm creeping on her or anything. I want to make sure she's okay with the secret-admirer stuff."

"Oh. Right." My stomach sank. "I'll . . . see what I can find out."

He paused as he caught the expression on my face, which must have been morose. "Hey . . ." He touched his hand to my arm. "You okay?"

I hesitated, thinking of the many ways in which I was *not* okay right now. I wanted to talk to him about Mom. I wanted to *not* have to deal with crushes and cheesy limericks. But I only had a few minutes to deliver the surprise to Kiya's locker *and* still make it to orchestra on time.

I straightened my shoulders. "Totally okay. Just in a hurry. See you at lunch."

Then I raced down the stairs and out into the crisp cold, resisting the urge to turn back and wave the way I always had before.

"Daniel wrote an actual *poem*?" Elle whispered as she stowed her French horn in her music locker. "Is this for real?"

I'd succeeded in taping the poem and flower to the outside of Kiya's locker without anybody seeing me. But I'd arrived in the orchestra room two minutes late, which had earned me a scolding look from Maestro Claudio. Then I'd spent every spare second of rehearsal texting Elle about Daniel and Kiya until Maestro Claudio confiscated my phone with a murmured, "This isn't like you, Ms. Durand. I'm surprised and disappointed."

Well, that made two of us. Nothing ever came between me and rehearsal, except, apparently, limericks.

Now I carefully put my cello in my own locker. "Sadly, yes. It's very real. And Daniel has a plan for other surprises, too. One for every day this week."

Elle shook her head in wonder. "I've got to hand it to Daniel. It's romantic."

I frowned as I slammed my locker shut.

"Nadi . . . you had to have seen this coming." Elle pulled her hair into a messy bun atop her head. "Whenever Kiya's around, Daniel can't take his eyes off her."

I winced. "But, Elle, we both heard Kiya talking about Graham . . ."

"I know." Elle shrugged. "Daniel can't help how he feels, though. We're just going to have to wait and see how the whole thing plays out."

"*Wait and see* isn't in my vocab," I said sullenly. "I don't do flexibility."

"No kidding." Elle laughed and pulled me into a hug. "It's going to be okay. And you're such a good BFF for helping him with his Prince Charming plan. We should be happy for him, right?"

I sighed. "It's just that Daniel and I are . . ." My voice died away in confusion.

Elle studied my face. "You and Daniel are what?" I shrugged. "Nadi, why *aren't* you happy for him?"

The question made my heart race, and confusion muddled my mind. "I don't know!" I blurted. "I guess I don't want to see him get hurt."

Elle pressed her lips together, like she was dying to say something but trying hard not to. At last she nodded. "Okay. If you say so." She glanced at her phone, then back at me. "I've got to go. Brandon's waiting at his locker. See you at lunch?"

I nodded glumly.

"Oh, and have fun convincing Maestro Claudio to give you back your phone!" she called with a wave over her shoulder.

"My phone," I groaned, remembering, and then collapsed against my locker. This day was getting better and better all the time.

"Really, Ms. Durand." Maestro Claudio tapped his baton against his palm in irritation. "Your audition is imminent, and yet you're preoccupied with this . . . instrument of mediocrity." He held my phone by his fingertips, as if touching such a device might give him a plague. "Take care you don't get heedless and squander this opportunity with Interlochen."

His dismal words followed me for the rest of the morning. And every time I thought about Kiya's poem, my stomach hurt. By lunchtime, all I wanted to do was sit down with Daniel, Elle, and Brandon and eat the way we used to—chatting easily about music and movies, complaining about pop quizzes and too much homework. But no sooner had I gotten into the lunch line than I caught sight of Kiya approaching with Georgette.

"Hey, Nadine!" she chirped enthusiastically. "How's your day been so far?"

"Great, thanks," I mumbled. I didn't want to hear about Kiya's poetic surprise, but it seemed that now I was stuck. "How's yours?"

"Kiya has a secret admirer," Georgette singsonged, giving Kiya a playfully teasing look. "He left a rose and a poem at her locker today."

"Georgette, could you have said that any louder?" Kiya

whispered, glancing around shyly at the other kids in line. "Not everyone needs to know."

Georgette laughed. "This is a small town. Everybody knows *everything* soon enough. Besides, this time of year, there's a sort of unspoken competition to see who can outdo who in the romantic gestures department. Kids around here make a huge deal out of Fall Formal invites," she explained knowingly. "Last year, one of the eighth graders asked someone to the dance by draping a hundred-foot banner in front of the school."

"Wow." Kiya smiled dreamily. "Nobody at my old school ever did anything like that."

"So you're cool with it?" I blurted. "I mean . . . the whole grandiose gesture thing? I'm sure the guy—whoever he is—would want you to be comfortable . . . He wouldn't want to be too forward or make you feel awkward."

Kiya nodded. "It's sweet. Besides, I have a sense that the guy . . . whoever he is . . . has good intentions. His poem . . ." She laughed. "Well, it was a little cheesy, but very cute."

"Well," Georgette said, "this so-called *secret* admirer's not much of a secret, if you ask me." She nodded toward a nearby table where Graham was sitting. Kiya laughed into her hand, blushing.

"Wait . . . you think Graham wrote the poem for you?" I asked Kiya.

Kiya dropped her gaze. "I'm not sure, but . . ."

"You hope so?" I asked softly.

"Maybe?" was her unsure response. But her excited smile was the answer I needed.

Relief was a cool breeze sweeping over me, but guilt quashed it a second later. How could I be wishing heartache on my BFF? How could I be happy about Kiya's interest in Graham when I knew it would hurt Daniel? It made me feel like a terrible person. It also made me not want to spend a minute longer in this lunch line with Kiya, for fear of hearing something else I might not want to have to tell Daniel later.

"I've got to go." I turned away from them so abruptly that I nearly tipped Kiya's tray with my own. "Sorry," I added as I hurried off.

Daniel could barely wait for me to sit down before he blurted, "Did she like the poem? What did she say?"

"Yeesh, Daniel." Elle shook her head. "Let Nadi breathe for a second."

"Don't look desperate, man," Brandon said to Daniel.

I laughed at that, but then saw Daniel's pleading look. "She loved the poem."

"Really?" Daniel's eyes lit up. "So she's okay with the surprises?"

"Yes." My palms were dampening, and I pressed them against the lunch bench. *Please don't ask any more questions*, I thought. I'd never lied to Daniel, and I didn't want to start now. But I didn't know how to tell him about Graham without hurting his feelings, either. It was better to avoid the topic entirely. "So that's it!" I blurted now. "That's everything."

"That's not even close to everything," Daniel said. "I already have an idea for tomorrow's surprise. It involves paper hearts . . ."

He went on, but the conversation receded into a distant hum. I didn't even hear my name being called until Daniel put his hand on my shoulder.

"Hey." He was peering at me, worry in his eyes. "Where'd you go just now? I looked over, and you were zombified."

"Nowhere." How could I explain that watching Daniel light up every time he mentioned Kiya made my stomach twist uncomfortably? How could I tell him that I wasn't happy about the idea of losing my best friend to a girlfriend? I couldn't. But there *was* something I could talk to him about, something that I'd been wanting to talk to him about all day. "Actually, there's been more drama with my mom."

"Really? When?"

"Last night, after you went home." I slid Mom's note from my back pocket. "Dad saw her, without telling me. And she wrote me this note—"

I started at the sound of the lunch bell. Like wind-up toys set in motion, everyone moved all at once—throwing away trash, picking up phones, heading for lockers.

"Wow, Nadi, that's huge. I want to hear the whole story . . ." Daniel said it sincerely, but his eyes were on Kiya as she walked out of the cafeteria. It wasn't until she was out of sight that he refocused his gaze on me. "Can we talk after school at the Mug?" He took the note from me and stuck it in his pocket, then stood to go. "I'll read it during study hall, and then tell you what I think over coffee later. Okay?"

He was already a dozen steps away, hurrying toward the door, probably in search of Kiya, by the time I managed a quiet "Okay."

"I'm going to need a double dose of Pumpkin Spice Supreme," I said to Elle as we made our way to the Snug Mug after school. We were walking past Pour Some Syrup on Me, Woodburn's homegrown maple-themed gift shop. The scent of sweet maple drifted out from its window. My stomach rumbled. "*And* a Nutella Banana Blitz waffle for good measure."

"Bad day?" She gave me a sideways glance before tucking her chin deeper into the collar of her coat.

I sighed. "I know Daniel likes Kiya, but I'm worried he's going a bit overboard."

"That's how he is. You know that."

I nodded. I *did* know that. But that didn't mean I was happy about it. "Maybe this is a phase. It could all blow over in a day or two."

I glanced at Elle, waiting for her to agree and make me feel better, but when we stepped into the Snug Mug, she stopped me. "Blow over?" Elle repeated. "I don't think so."

I followed her gaze, and saw Daniel and Kiya side by side behind the counter, laughing and chatting. My stomach churned, and I instantly thought about backtracking out of the shop, not wanting to witness a flirt-a-thon. But then Daniel's eyes lit on me, and he was by my side in a blink, whispering in my ear, "Code Red. Upstairs. Be there in five."

I dumped my cello and school stuff on the floor beside Elle, who had already taken up her spot on our fave papasan chair. I saw Graham breeze through the door of the shop, and an instant later, Kiya waved at him from behind the counter.

Graham started to get in line, which was so long in the after-school rush that it almost reached the door. Before he had the chance, Kiya rushed over to him.

"You don't have to wait in line." She offered him a flirty smile.

"I'll bring your drink out right away. Just tell me what you want."

"Whiteout Chocolatta," Graham said. "You're awesome. Thanks."

Kiya pressed her hand onto his arm, giving him a longer look. "No. Thank *you*."

Graham looked momentarily confused as she walked away, and I wondered if he'd even heard yet about the poem he'd *supposedly* written for her. Still, he looked thrilled to be getting special treatment from Kiya.

I climbed the stairs to the loft and sank into the couch, trying to settle my overwrought nerves. It was only when Daniel appeared with a Pumpkin Spice Supreme and my Nutella Banana Blitz waffle that I felt a loosening of some of the tension I'd felt all day.

"How did you know I needed this?" I said, taking a long sip of coffee.

He smiled. "I read your mom's note, for starters."

"Oh." So he *had* been paying attention when he'd taken the

note at lunch today. My mood lifted slightly. "Yup. It was kind of a shock."

"That she wrote it, or that your dad went to see her and didn't tell you about it?"

I paused, trying to decide. "Both. All of it." I took a deep breath, and told him about the conversation I'd had with my dad last night. "It seems so surreal, you know? I've only ever really known her on paper. I can't even imagine what she's like in real life."

Daniel nodded. "I think that about my dad all the time. I know him from his photos, but people are so much more than that in reality. The thing is, Nadi . . ." He held my gaze. "You don't have to imagine your mom anymore. You could actually see her."

I blinked. "Wait . . . you think I *should* see her?"

Daniel's expression told me that he wanted to tread carefully. "I could never tell you what you should do. But if it were me in your place . . ." He took a deep breath. "I think I'd agree to see her. Yeah."

I stared into the whipped cream of my Pumpkin Spice Supreme. My drink seemed about as appetizing now as curdled milk. I set my cup down, then slid it even farther away so I wouldn't have to look at it anymore.

"What's wrong?" Daniel glanced at the cup. "Did I put soy milk in again?"

"It's not that." I shook my head. "I thought you were on my side. Always."

"I *am*!" Daniel held up his hands. "Hey . . . if you didn't want me to tell you what I thought, why did you ask me to read the note?"

I groaned in exasperation. "Because I was hoping that you'd say it was okay for me to keep ignoring my mom. But you're not going to, are you?"

He smiled gently. "I plead the fifth."

"Ugh!" I flopped back against the couch. "You know what? I wish my mom had just shown up unannounced on the doorstep. Then I wouldn't even have to deal with this decision, or this note. I could've slammed the door in her face and been done with it."

Daniel cocked his head at me. "Would you really have done it?"

I opened my mouth to spit out the first word that came into my mind. *Yes!* I wanted to shout. But the word wouldn't come, and a second later, Kiya's singsong voice was calling for Daniel from downstairs.

Daniel peered over the railing at Kiya, his beaming smile too much for me to bear. "What's up?" he asked her.

"I need some help with the register," Kiya said. "I've never had to put in a discount, and we've got the half-price specialty drinks today."

"I'll be right there." Daniel headed for the stairs. "Oh." He glanced back at me in surprise, as if, the moment he'd heard Kiya's voice, he'd forgotten I was there entirely. "To be continued tomorrow?"

"You're not coming over for dinner tonight?" I asked.

He shook his head, grinning. "I've got to brainstorm surprises."

Then he was down the steps without another word. I lifted my Pumpkin Spice Supreme to my lips, hoping that, even if I wasn't craving it the way I usually did, another sip might still bring me the cozy comfort I needed. The nutmeg and cinnamon sweetness glided over my tongue, but all I tasted was the wrongness of this day. I couldn't take one more sip.

Chapter Eight

My phone buzzed for the third time in five minutes. I resisted the urge to throttle it, reminding myself that it was not the phone that was the cause of my frustration. It was Daniel.

Last night, I'd texted him just before bed, telling him that I hadn't been able to practice cello at all. I'd tried to work on my audition piece, but I flubbed the same measures over and over again, until I panicked and then gave up entirely. I hadn't heard back from Daniel until this morning, but when he finally texted, it was only to offer a quick apology for being so busy with Operation Kiya, and that we'd talk more at school.

Apparently, Daniel's version of talking was texting nonstop to ask for updates. I glanced at the screen now, trying to keep it hidden from Ms. Bronski, my homeroom teacher.

Any sign of Ruby yet? Daniel's text read.

My thumbs punched the screen as I typed a definitive NO for the third time. But just as I hit send, Ruby, our school's resident therapy dog, rounded the corner to our classroom. Ruby visited our class once or twice a week as she made her daily rounds through the school. Sometimes she curled up at students' feet when they were taking tests, or napped in the corner of a classroom while we learned. Today, though, as I guessed from the small teal-green box tied to her harness, Ruby had a different job entirely.

Ms. Bronski greeted Ruby with a head scratch before bending down to inspect the gift on her back. "What's this you have here?" Ms. Bronski read the gift tag, then straightened, giving a disgruntled sniff, and said, "Ms. Renaud. It appears you have received a package."

All eyes turned toward Kiya, who was blinking with an

innocent *Who, me?* expression. She grinned and walked to the front of the room, saying happily, "I honestly have no idea what this is about."

After retrieving the box, she sat back down at her desk and lifted the lid. The bottom of the box popped open, revealing 3-D hearts and tiny Cupid-shaped confetti. Inside the box were written the words: *When you smile, you knock me out, I fall apart, and I thought I was so smart.*

"Aw . . . how sweet!" Kiya cooed. "It's a quote from *Hamilton*."

"Your favorite musical." Georgette leaned toward Kiya conspiratorially. "He knows you so well."

I tried not to roll my eyes. As Ms. Bronski finished the morning's announcements, I quickly typed a text to Daniel, saying, Mission accomplished. The bell rang a few minutes later, and I walked out of the classroom, relieved that I wouldn't have to give any more "Operation Kiya" reports today. I had enough on my mind as it was.

Then Kiya called my name, and I saw her hurrying down the hallway toward me.

"Hey, Nadine." She smiled breathlessly as she fell into step beside me. "Can we talk for a sec?"

"Sure," I said hesitantly. What was this about?

She put her hand on my arm to slow my stride, then stopped to face me. "Have I . . . done something to make you mad at me?"

My mouth dropped open. I hadn't been expecting that.

"I feel like you don't really like me," Kiya went on, "and I'm not sure if I offended you somehow—"

Oh gosh. I hadn't realized I'd been coming off as overtly hostile to Kiya. Were my mixed emotions that obvious?

"You didn't offend me," I said, feeling guilty. "Really."

She smiled in relief. "Whew. For a second, I thought maybe you were crushing on Graham, too?"

My eyes widened. "Wha—? No. Not at all," I said.

"Oh good." She let out a long breath. "That would've been totally awkward and awful." She tilted her head at me. "But . . . is there something else? I feel like there's this weird tension between us."

I bit my lip. There was so much I wasn't capable of telling her. I had no explanation for why I couldn't warm up to her. I didn't understand it myself. One thing, though, did pop into my head, and suddenly, I saw a chance to change the subject *and* make a point, all at once.

"Well, if I'm being totally honest, I'm not a huge fan of the menu changing at the Snug Mug," I said. "And I'm not the only one." I'd heard kids complaining about the menu changes in the hallway before school had started today.

"Really?" Her brow crinkled.

I shrugged. "Kids here love the specialty drinks. Including Graham."

"He does love the Whiteout Chocolatta," she said thoughtfully. "But my dad's already made up his mind. And honestly, those fancy drinks are tasty, but also loaded with sugar. The new drinks are healthier anyway." She checked the time on her phone. "I've got to go." She started to walk away, then turned back, giving me a quizzical look. "You don't . . . you don't know who my secret admirer is, do you? *Is* it Graham?"

My pulse stuttered, but I shook my head, replying, "Absolutely no idea."

Then she was gone, and my phone was buzzing with yet another text from Daniel, asking me to meet him at his locker. I sighed, guessing he wanted another Kiya update. Sure enough, when I reached his locker, I found him pacing in anticipation.

"Yes, she was thrilled," I said preemptively, hoping to ward off the onslaught of questions.

"Great! Two surprises down, only three more to go." His expression was gleeful. "And tomorrow night's serenade is going to be the best yet!"

I raised a skeptical eyebrow. "Daniel, *don't* tell me you're going to sing under her window?"

He shook his head. "But I *do* have some live entertainment in mind." The mischievous glint in his eyes already had me worried, but then he added, "See, I know some really talented musicians—"

"No *way*." I cut him off. "Whatever it is you're about to ask me to do is *not* going to happen."

"Elle's already on board," Daniel said, "but I can't have a French horn without a cello. You're the star of the show."

I sighed, unable to meet his eyes. "Daniel, I'm not even close to ready for my audition. I can't give up a night of practice to serenade—" *Some stupid crush*, I wanted to say, but held the words back. "I can't," I repeated instead. "Really."

There was an awkward beat of silence before he said, quietly, "I'm sorry, Nadi. I didn't mean to pressure you. I'll figure something else out." Suddenly, I saw how much this meant to him. Regardless of how much his fawning over Kiya irritated *me*, this was important to *him*. We'd been through so much together. I couldn't let him down.

I threw up my hands. "Ugh! Okay, okay. I'll do it."

He grabbed me in a hug, and suddenly, my breath left my body. "What would I do without you, Nadi?" Even when he let go, the warmth of his arms lingered.

"I'm all yours," I blurted. The second the words left my mouth, I froze, mortified. Daniel's eyes widened in surprise. "N-no," I stammered. "I mean—"

Daniel laughed. "I know what you meant. I'd do anything for you, too."

"I've got to get to class," I mumbled, walking away from him. "Just . . . fill me in on the details for the serenade later."

"Thanks!" he called cheerily after me.

I barreled down the hallway, still dazed by my strange response to his hug. I wasn't supposed to go breathless around him. Daniel was my friend, and he was soon to be Kiya's boyfriend. And—stupid me—I'd even offered to help him win her over. What had I gotten myself into?

As it turned out, what I'd gotten myself into was climbing a tree in the dead of night.

"You're going to break your leg." Elle's whispered voice sounded in the darkness below.

I strengthened my grip on the sturdy (hopefully) tree branch and pulled myself up. "Thanks for that vote of confidence," I hissed. I was grateful for Wednesday's moonless night, which kept me from seeing just how far I'd fall if I slipped.

"I can't believe we agreed to this," Elle said.

"No kidding," I muttered.

I shimmied forward on the branch a few more inches, thankful that the knapsack on my back was relatively light. Then, when I was near enough to Kiya's bedroom window that I could reach the sill, I opened the knapsack. Inside was the battery-operated light-up rose that Daniel had "borrowed" from the school drama club's supply closet. I switched it on and carefully set it on the windowsill, where it twinkled with fiber optic color-changing lights.

Luckily, Kiya's curtains were drawn, so I didn't have to worry about her seeing it (or me) before Elle and I had the rest of the surprise ready. I quickly clambered back down the tree and then found Elle waiting with our instruments behind some hedges.

I swept the blanket off my cello, hoping that it hadn't gotten too cold, and extended the pin on the bottom to its full height, so that I could play standing up.

"Ready?" I asked Elle. She lifted her French horn to her lips and nodded.

"On three," I whispered, and counted off.

Daniel had chosen the song, John Legend's "All of Me," and it hadn't taken Elle and me much time to put together an arrangement for our duet. I'd always been able to quickly pick up and play songs by ear, and Elle was a master at accompaniment.

Now, our music floated through the brisk air, traveling up into the night.

It only took a few seconds for Kiya's bedroom light to come on. She drew her curtains aside and opened her window. I saw her smile as she examined the glowing rose, and then she leaned out the window, trying to find the source of the music.

I picked up speed in the last few measures of the song, wanting to finish and leave before Kiya, or anyone else, came out of her house. But I wasn't quick enough. As I was zipping my cello back into its case, the Renauds' front porch light blinked on. Kiya stepped onto the porch, peering into the darkness.

"Hello out there," she called and waited. "Graham," she whispered, "is it you?"

"Elle," I hissed, pulling on my friend's arm as she stifled a nervous giggle, "we've got to go. Now!"

We stumbled across the uneven ground, strewn as it was with fallen leaves.

"That was amazing!" Kiya called after us as we ran. "I wish I could tell you that face-to-face!"

While I was bemoaning the fact that Woodburn had gravel and dirt paths between houses instead of sidewalks, I was still grateful for the town's lack of streetlights. The darkness kept us hidden until we made it safely back to Main Street.

"Please tell me I don't ever have to do that again," Elle panted when we finally stopped at the corner where we would part ways to head home. "Running with a French horn is no picnic."

"You should try it with a cello." Even with my cello in its padded backpack-style case, I'd have to check it when I got home to make sure it had survived our narrow escape unscathed. Just then, my phone buzzed with a text from Daniel, wanting to know how our Music in the Moonlight Mission (as he called it) had gone. "Hang on a sec," I said to Elle while I sent a text back saying I'd call him in a few to fill him in.

"How many more of these Operation Kiya missions are you helping with, anyway?" Elle asked.

"I don't want to talk about it," I muttered, then added, "I don't suppose you want to come over to help me cut out paper hearts? I told Dan I'd cut out half of them for him. They're for tomorrow morning's mission."

Elle laughed. "I don't even think I'd do that for my *boyfriend*, let alone my BFF's crush. I mean, we all love Daniel, but you're really going above and beyond for him."

My face warmed at her words, and I felt her studying me. "I want him to be happy," I said softly, and I knew it was true. Even though the thought of Kiya and Daniel together made a hollow pit form in my stomach, I didn't want Daniel to miss out on anything he wanted.

"Nadi . . . you and Daniel have been friends forever," Elle said now, "but . . . well, you know you can talk to me if anything changes."

"What? You mean when Daniel's grand scheme works and Kiya falls for him?" I wrinkled my nose.

"I wasn't thinking about Kiya," she said, so softly I wasn't even sure I'd heard her right. Then she gave me a lightning-quick hug and hurried in the direction of her house, leaving me staring after her, wondering what she'd meant.

"Are you sure you put the drone in the right place?" Daniel asked as he met me at our lunch table on Friday afternoon. "You should double-check, because if it's in the wrong place, the signal won't reach and—"

"I'm not double-checking." I'd practically had to run from my locker to the cafeteria in order to get there before any of the other students arrived for lunch. I'd strategically placed the drone, with its precious cargo, around the corner from the cafeteria entrance in an out-of-sight spot. I'd done enough. "If this one surprise doesn't work, it's not the end of the world."

"But it's the last one. It has to be perfect." Daniel grinned at me as he retrieved the drone's remote control from his backpack. "This is the best one yet, don't you think?"

I hesitated, torn by a mix of emotions. This final mission was the most elaborate so far. "It's definitely creative," I conceded, trying to sound as diplomatic as possible.

My reticent tone didn't fool him for a second.

"What's wrong?" he asked, his brow creasing with concern. "You think it's stupid?"

I groaned inwardly. Daniel and I had spent hours prepping for and executing the last few Operation Kiya missions. Thursday, I'd gotten to school before orchestra rehearsal to slip paper hearts through Kiya's locker vents, until her locker was filled with one hundred hearts that waterfalled out when she opened the locker door. And now this. I was *so* done with Operation Kiya, and I wanted Daniel to be done with it, too. He wasn't the one in Kiya's homeroom listening to her whisper to Georgette about Graham. He hadn't noticed how Kiya skipped spots in the lunch line so she could talk to Graham. But I had.

It was obvious that Kiya had fallen for Graham. Or it was obvious to everyone *except* Daniel. But as I looked at him now—at the hope and disappointment seesawing on his face—I knew I couldn't tell him about Graham. It would crush him.

"Daniel," I said gently. "The drone idea *isn't* stupid. It's cool." I swallowed. The cafeteria was still pretty empty, with kids just beginning to trickle in, so we had a minute or two to talk in relative privacy. "It's only . . . you're spending so much time and energy on Kiya. A girl who . . ." I sucked in a breath. "You barely know."

"It takes time to get to know someone. I mean, come on." He looked at me with that smile I knew oh so well, and my heart filled with warmth. "You can't expect me to know everything about her yet. It's not like you and me! Nothing comes as easy as that." He paused, laughing. "That's not what I meant. I mean, that *is* what I meant, but—"

"I get it, Daniel." I laughed, too, but my pulse pounded furiously. "Of course it's not like you and me." I glanced away from him in order to hide my reddening cheeks, and at that moment, spotted Brandon and Elle making their way toward our table. It was perfect timing. "I'm going to go grab lunch," I said, scrambling toward the hot lunch line before he could say anything else.

Once I got in line, I pressed my palms against my cool steel lunch tray. *This is Daniel*, I reminded myself. I was not supposed to become light-headed over Daniel. What was wrong with me?

I wished I didn't have to watch the surprise about to unfold for Kiya. But as I turned from the lunch line with my now-full tray of food, I caught sight of Kiya sitting down at her table with Georgette.

Within seconds, Daniel's mini drone, carrying a small pink pouch, flew into the room and straight toward Kiya. Amid awestruck "oohs" from nearly everyone in the room, the drone released the pink pouch, and it landed with a soft *plop* right in front of Kiya. The drone flew deftly away as Kiya beamed over her special delivery.

"What is this?" she cried in delight. Georgette and all the other girls at the table leaned forward to see. Kiya pulled the strings on the pouch and up popped a miniature paper silhouette of New York City. "Omigod, that's the cutest thing ever!" she gushed.

My stomach lurched as I slowly made my way past Kiya's table and back to my friends. When I sat down beside Daniel again, he was beaming.

"Impressive, man." Brandon nodded approvingly. "How did you swing that one?"

"Paper, scissors, Pinterest. And this." Daniel held open the front pocket of his hoodie to reveal the drone's remote control he'd hidden inside it.

My throat had gone completely dry, and suddenly, my lunch seemed inedible. While Brandon and Elle asked Daniel more questions about his paper engineering skills, I glanced in Kiya's direction. She was still smiling, marveling over Daniel's craftmanship.

Suddenly, I couldn't watch anymore. I couldn't be here at all.

I stood, accidentally banging my tray against the table. "I'm going to the music room. Get some practice time in."

My three friends looked up in surprise, and Elle's eyes momentarily caught mine in a look of concern.

"Oh . . . okay." Daniel's tone was disappointed, but I couldn't care about that right now. "See you after school?"

I nodded, then hurried away before they could ask any more questions.

My clunky, mistake-riddled practicing (and Maestro Claudio's disgruntled tsking as he listened from his office) over the next half hour did nothing to improve my mood. I'd grown accustomed to the maestro's taskmaster attitude over the last three years. I even considered his tough standard a challenge I could rise to. To earn his stern nod of approval after a particularly inspired rehearsal made me happy. There was no nod from him today, though, only a fretful scowl as he poked his head in to check on me.

What Maestro Claudio didn't know was that, whenever I drew the bow across the strings, Daniel's face appeared before my eyes. And then—even worse—Kiya's face appeared beside his, closing in for a kiss. After nearly launching my bow across the room, I gave up entirely and packed up my cello. I was about to leave when the sound of voices in the hallway caught my attention.

I cautiously peered around the doorway to see Kiya and Graham standing in the hall together.

"I've been wanting to talk to you," Kiya was saying to him. She twirled a lock of her hair slowly around her finger, glancing up at Graham with wide, sparkling eyes and a flirty smile.

"Then I guess this is my lucky day," Graham said.

"Would you like to go see the Big Pumpkin Blaze with me?" She asked the question without so much as a single falter, and I found myself admiring her bravery. "Maybe sometime this weekend? I haven't been yet. I know it's sort of a touristy thing to do, but it sounds really cool."

He grinned. "It *is* cool, until you go a hundred times. After that, it's sort of like, been there, done that." He laughed. "But sure, I'll go with you. I'm glad you asked."

"Well, you dropped enough clues that you're interested, so . . ." Her smile broadened.

Omigod. I clenched my fists, remembering what Kiya had said earlier about thinking the surprise gifts she'd been getting were from Graham. She *still* thought he was her secret admirer! I glanced at Graham, thinking that he'd surely understand and tell her that the gifts weren't from him.

For a millisecond, Graham's expression blanked, but he recovered smoothly. "Yeah, I was hoping you'd figure it out sooner or later. I thought we had a moment in the coffee shop the other day."

I leaned against the wall, my thoughts reeling. Here Graham was thinking he'd won Kiya over with his good looks and charm, and Kiya was thinking he'd just confessed to being her secret admirer. What a disaster!

"Hey, there's a party at Liam's house tonight," Graham added. "We could go to the Blaze for about an hour or so, and then go to the party."

"Perfect," I heard Kiya say, and then the bell rang. I waited out of sight in the music room while they exchanged phone numbers, and then slowly made my way down the hallway, stunned, panicked, and relieved all at once.

Kiya and Graham had a date. This made me happy, but also—oh no—made me feel terrible for Daniel. All the work he'd put into Operation Kiya had been for nothing, and now he was going to have to come to terms with Kiya dating Graham. It was going to be awful.

There was only one person who could break the news to him. Someone who'd do it gently and properly, before the Woodburn gossip reached him. It was going to have to be me.

Chapter Nine

The second the last bell rang, I raced to my locker, phone in hand, ready to text Daniel with a Code Red. My fingers froze over the screen, though, when I glanced up to see a piece of paper, folded into the shape of a music note, taped to my locker. I unfolded it and read:

Nadi,
    I know we haven't been able to hang out as much lately, and I'm sorry. I've been distracted, but I miss you. I want to thank you for everything you've done to help me this

week. Meet me at the Snug Mug ASAP after
school. I have a surprise for you that you'll
LOVE.

Daniel

My heart sprang happily in my chest. Had Daniel been missing me as much as I'd been missing him? The thought warmed me from the inside out, and after grabbing my cello from the music room, I was flying down the school steps and onto Main Street, my eyes glued to the Snug Mug's A-frame roof in the distance.

I blew through the door of the Mug, an expectant smile on my face, my eyes scanning the room for Daniel and whatever fun surprise he had planned for me.

But I didn't see Daniel anywhere, only Elle and Brandon tucked into the papasan chair. When Elle caught sight of me, she looked strangely sheepish, even concerned.

"Nadi . . ." She stood up and started toward me. "There's someone he—"

"Nadi!" Daniel's voice drowned out Elle's, and I glanced up to see him waving from the Mug's loft. His face was lit with the excitement it always had when he'd masterminded a surprise he was particularly proud of. "Up here!"

I couldn't wait another moment and sprang up the steps, taking them two at a time, ignoring Elle's pleading, "Wait!" My one fleeting thought as my foot hit the final step was: *Why is Elle telling me to wait?*

Then I understood. Standing at the top of the stairs was my mother.

My body turned statue-still. Somewhere far beneath the roar of my pulse, I heard Daniel's muffled, "Surprise!" But I couldn't speak or move. All I could do was stare.

Mom's face looked older than I remembered, with some new, faint lines etched around her eyes and the corners of her mouth. She'd colored the tips of her wavy brown hair purple, and she wore a long, belted dress and slouchy boots.

"Nadine!" Mom exclaimed with a smile, and threw her arms around me in a fierce hug. "I can't believe how tall you are! And your hair's so much longer." She swiped at her eyes with one hand without loosening her hold on me with the other. "I've been waiting for this for so long, and now here you are. It doesn't even seem real!"

My arms were stiff against my sides, and I didn't make a move to return her embrace. My neck was damp with her tears, but as she pressed her hands against my cheeks and ran them over my hair, I stood, still frozen. Panic avalanched down my back.

I glanced at Daniel, thinking he'd see the distress in my eyes and help.

But Daniel was beaming at Mom and me, oblivious to my growing agitation. "This is so great," he was gushing. "I knew it would work. And everybody's so happy—"

"No." My voice was strangled by the nerves tightening every fiber of my being. "No!" I cried, louder this time, directing my words at Mom. "You think you can hug me like you did when I was a baby and that will make everything okay?"

In the faint distance, I registered the shop's chatter quiet below.

I yanked free of Mom's arms, and her radiant smile dimmed into confusion. "Wh-what are you doing here?" I blustered. "I never said that you could come, and you . . . you show up out of nowhere!"

Mom glanced at Daniel uncertainly, and then back at me, her cheeks paling. "I thought . . . we thought . . ." She took two steps back, her hands falling limply to her sides.

"What? That you could blindside me and I'd be okay with it?" I turned to Daniel now, whose expression looked nearly as stricken as Mom's. Behind him on the coffee table sat two untouched mugs of Pumpkin Spice Supreme and a vase of flowers. "You set this whole thing up without telling me?" I gestured toward the table, where he'd probably envisioned Mom and me bonding over a newly discovered shared love for pumpkin spice. "And you thought I'd be *happy* about it?"

Daniel opened his mouth, but Mom interjected before he could say anything. "I'm so sorry," she whispered hoarsely. "I didn't know . . . I thought you wanted this. When Daniel reached out to me, I assumed it was because you'd asked him to. I never would've come if I'd known you hadn't agreed to it. I . . ." Her voice broke, and her eyes filled. "I'll go."

Her last two words were barely audible as she stepped past me and hurried down the stairs, unsteadily clutching the banister as she went.

I caught a quick glimpse of Brandon, down below, opening the door for Mom as she stumbled through it, and Elle looking up at me worriedly. But then I was whirling to face Daniel.

"How could you ever think that having my mom show up here unannounced was a good idea?" My voice quavered.

"Nadi, please don't be angry," he started. "I thought you'd be happy. That if you saw her in person, you'd change your mind, and—"

"You didn't think," I snapped. "You never do when you're fixated on one of your grandiose ideas. You fantasize about these great surprises, but you don't *think*!"

"Come on, Nadi, she's your *mom*," he continued, as if none of what I'd said had sunk in at all. "It's obvious that she loves you, and you have a chance at a relationship with her. Why *wouldn't* you want that?"

"Because she left!" I cried. "Because she didn't care enough to be around for the last six years." I threw up my hands. "I don't have to give you reasons, because it's *my* decision. *Not* yours. And you took it away from me!"

Daniel shook his head. "Sometimes life doesn't give you second chances . . ." His voice softened, and there was longing on his face as he spoke. "But you have one. You should take it."

"Don't tell me what to do." I glared at him. "You should've stayed out of it. Your stupid surprises never work anyway. Not with me, and *definitely* not with Kiya."

He frowned, confusion in his eyes. "What do you mean? Kiya's loved every one of the surprises—"

"She thinks they're from Graham!" I blurted.

His eyes widened. "What?"

"She's crushing on Graham." I nodded as he shook his head in disbelief. "She's giving him all the credit for the gifts you gave

156

her. She thinks he's her secret admirer. And he likes her, too. They're going on a date tonight."

"No." Daniel's voice was firm with denial. "That can't be right . . ."

"If you would quit living in a daydream all the time, you'd see it. I wanted to tell you earlier this week but—"

"It doesn't matter." Daniel's tone was already hopeful again. "Graham's not right for Kiya, and once she realizes it, I'll be here waiting. I'm not giving up."

I threw my head back in frustration. "God, don't you even hear what I'm saying?" I met his eyes, and felt all the irritation inside me pouring out. "No, you don't. You want to keep living in your pretend world of happy endings and perfect reunions, and—and you never stop to think about who you're hurting!" I turned for the stairs. "I'm done helping you with your projects. I'm done with everything."

"Nadi, wait," Daniel pleaded. "Today wasn't supposed to go like this . . ."

His voice faded as I ran down the stairs, past the stares of Elle,

Brandon, and most of the other customers in the Snug Mug, and out the door.

The frigid air stung my eyes as I ran, and tears poured down my cheeks. I wanted to run until the hurt faces of Mom and Daniel were obliterated from my memory forever. But no amount of running could erase them from my mind.

I didn't expect Dad to be home when I burst into our house, my cheeks red and raw with tears. But I found him sitting on the sofa in the living room, a distraught expression on his face.

"You saw your mother, then," he said matter-of-factly, as if he'd been fearing or expecting this all along.

"You—you know what happened?" I stammered. "How—"

"She stopped in here before she went to the Snug Mug." He clasped and unclasped his hands, avoiding my eyes. He took a deep breath. "I knew she was coming today."

"*You* knew, too?" I cried. "Am I the only one who didn't know?" I clenched my eyes shut against the memory of Elle, trying to stop me as I came in the door of the Snug Mug. She'd probably been trying to warn me, maybe give me a few seconds, at least, to mentally prepare.

Dad stood up and started toward me. But he hesitated when he saw my tear-streaked face, the crying too daunting for him to handle.

"Daniel asked me about setting up the meeting with your mom." Dad shrugged. "He thought it would be better to surprise you with a visit, and that way you wouldn't have time to overthink it."

"And you let him plan it?" I stared at him. "You're my *dad*! You shouldn't have let one of my friends get involved in this. This was between you, me, and Mom!"

Dad ran a hand through his hair. "You and Daniel are so close. He knows you so well. I thought—"

"You thought that Daniel knew me better than you did, so you'd let him decide, so you wouldn't have to." My eyes brimmed afresh.

"Nadine. That's not what I thought," Dad said. "I should've told you beforehand. It was wrong to spring this on you. I see that now."

"You should've told me!" I cried. "But you never tell me anything. Living with you is like living alone! I never know how you feel about anything."

Dad's eyes drooped at their corners, and his mouth sagged in sadness. "I didn't know you felt that way." His tone was surprised. "You've always been so independent and self-sufficient. You never needed me for much of anything after your mom left, so I thought you were okay . . ."

"You should've asked!" I exclaimed. "Or not asked, but just . . . played board games with me anyway! Or built the pillow fort . . . or whatever. Don't assume I'm okay because I handle things on my own. Maybe I *want* to be taken care of—sort of—" My voice dropped, and I added an awkward, "A little bit every now and then."

Dad's face tucked in on itself, and I sighed. The rabbit was retreating into his warren.

"Forget it." My voice wobbled and, within seconds, tears were leaking from my eyes again. "This whole day's been a mistake. Just do me a favor?" My voice was squeaky with crying now.

"If Mom calls, I don't want to talk to her. You deal with it. Or don't." I turned for my bedroom stairs. "I don't care either way."

I wasn't getting out of bed. That's what I decided on Saturday when I woke up and the memory of Friday's disaster hit me like a sledgehammer right between the eyes. I squinted at my phone's screen and found seven new voice mails (all from Daniel) and thirty new text messages (all from Elle). The texts ranged from Call me to Hello? to the last one, sent at noon: I'm coming over whether you like it or not!

I deleted Daniel's messages without listening to them, then pulled the blanket over my head, determined to shut out the world. No such luck, because a moment later Dad's voice called my name. I pulled the blanket tighter around me.

"I have to run to the grocery store," Dad said, and I guessed by the nearness of his voice that he was at the top of my bedroom stairs, debating whether to come all the way up or not. "Do you need anything?" When I didn't answer, I heard a muffled sigh. "Okay, then. I made you some grilled cheese and tomato soup.

We need a break from chili, don't you think? It's on the kitchen table when you're ready."

His feet creaked on the stairs, and I thought he'd gone, but then his voice came again.

"I talked to your mom last night."

I already knew he had. I'd heard the phone ring, and could tell from the tone of his voice who he was talking to. I hadn't been able to make out what he was saying, though, and now I held my breath, waiting.

"No one's going to pressure you to do anything, Nadi," Dad said now. "You only have to see your mom again if you feel ready. I promise." There was a pause, and then, "We *both* promise."

His steps retreated down the stairs, and a few minutes later I heard the front door click open and shut. I snuggled down deeper into the covers, not wanting to acknowledge the sunlight streaming through my window, or the fact that it was a new day at all.

I had just started dozing again when the weight of someone sitting down on my bed made me yelp.

"If you ever want to see your cello again," Elle's voice said, "hand over the ransom money now."

"My cello!" I tried to throw off the covers but got hopelessly tangled in them instead. "Omigod, I left it at the Snug Mug yesterday afternoon!" I yanked at the covers until I freed myself, then found Elle sitting complacently at the foot of my bed, my cello case cradled in her arms, my schoolbag (which I'd also left) at her feet. I instinctively reached for the case, but she swung it away from me teasingly. "No ransom money?" she asked, and when I didn't answer, she shrugged. "I'd settle for chocolate instead."

I flopped back against the pillow. "Thank you for rescuing my cello."

She grabbed me in a big hug. "I'm so sorry that Daniel sprang your mom on you like that. I swear I didn't know about it until I got to the Mug. And then she was . . . *there*! If I'd known beforehand, I would've tried to stop Daniel."

I sighed. "It's okay. I . . . don't want to talk about it, okay?"

She nodded. "Okay."

"And I'm *not* leaving my bed. Ever."

"Fine." She tried to lighten the mood by feigning nonchalance. "Then I guess you don't want to hear about the Kiya-Graham scandal last night, either."

"What now? They're eloping to Switzerland to ski the Alps?"

Elle smiled, shaking her head. "Rumor has it that they're finito, after dating for less than twelve hours. That has to be a record." She lay across the foot of my bed, clearly relishing the fact that she had the scoop. "Apparently, Graham kissed Heather while he was at a party with Kiya last night. They were playing spin the bottle, but Kiya didn't care why it happened. She told Graham that she won't waste her time on a guy who kisses other girls on some whim."

I rolled my eyes and groaned. "And this is supposed to cheer me up *how?*"

"I know you're not a huge Kiya fan, so I thought you might get a little satisfaction out of hearing that she doesn't always get everything she wants." She scanned my frowning face. "Nope. I guess not."

"I'm not evil, Elle. I'm not going to cheer because Kiya was treated badly. She might be annoyingly perfect, but I don't hate her. I just don't want her dating—" I caught myself when I realized that I was about to say "Daniel." I didn't even want to *think* his name right now, but there was something else, too. *Why* didn't I want Kiya dating Daniel? The question made me squirm.

"Who?" Elle perked up, resting her head in her cupped palms. "*Who* don't you want her dating?"

"Never mind," I mumbled, not wanting to pin down whatever was making my pulse surge. I tried yanking the covers back over my head, but I was foiled when Elle pinned them down.

"Nadi, I know you're upset about yesterday. Daniel overstepped. Way, *way* overstepped. But he never meant to hurt you. And the situation with your mom—"

"Don't." I cut her off. "I already told you I don't want to talk about it."

"It stinks," she said. "That's all I was going to say. The situation with your mom stinks." She reached for my hand. "I'm here for you if you want to talk about it. Anytime."

My lip trembled. "Thanks," I managed to whisper.

She hugged me again, then nodded to my cello. "How's your audition practice coming along, anyway?"

I groaned. "Don't ask."

Elle held up her hands. "Sorry," she said. Then, after a few seconds, she added, "Brandon and I are going pumpkin picking with—um, with Daniel. We're heading out in a little bit. Wanna come? It might make you feel better."

I shook my head. "I don't want to see him," I said quietly.

Elle opened her mouth like she wanted to say more, then closed it, standing up. "Text if you change your mind." At the stairs, she turned back to me. "How does that saying go? People are always hardest on the ones they hate the most."

"It's love," I corrected her. "People are always hardest on the ones they love the most."

"Right. That's it." She blew me a kiss. "Well . . . good luck practicing."

She was down the stairs and out the door before I even caught on to the little mind trick she'd played on me. Well, if she thought I was being too hard on Daniel, she was wrong. I burrowed under the covers again. I wasn't about to let him off the hook. No way.

Chapter Ten

"Ms. Durand." Maestro Claudio was leaning over my music stand. "*Where* is your head?"

"I—I'm sorry." I lifted my bow to the strings of my cello, preparing to run through the three measures I'd been struggling with. "I'm ready now."

"No." In the maestro's frown, I saw the truth I already felt in my heart. I'd felt it this weekend each time I picked up my cello, only to find my fingers slipping, my bow screeching unearthly howls instead of heavenly music. I *wasn't* ready. Not for this early-Monday-morning practice session, and certainly not for

Thursday's Interlochen audition. "Ms. Durand," the maestro continued now, "I am deeply concerned about your performance. I wonder if you understand the gravity of your situation."

I nodded miserably. "My audition is Thursday."

"Indeed. The audition will not go well if you do not fix this problem." He tapped his baton against his palm. "You emailed me last night, asking for help fine-tuning your audition pieces. *This*"—he tapped the music on my stand with his baton—"is not fine-tuning. This is a screaming banshee."

I hung my head. "I don't know what's wrong," I mumbled. "It's like I've lost the ability to play. It all sounds awful. Maybe . . . maybe I'm burned out."

"Do not utter such nonsense in my presence." He spun away from me in irritation. "For great musicians, there is no such thing as burnout. There is only . . ." This time, he tapped the baton against his temple. "The musical psyche." He turned back to me and scrutinized my face. "When the mind is muddled, the playing is muddled."

"But—" I was about to tell him my mind wasn't muddled,

then stopped. I knew perfectly well that wasn't true. I'd spent the entire weekend tormenting myself about Mom, or Daniel, or both. Half the time, I couldn't even pinpoint what emotions I was feeling; they ranged from devastated to irate and beyond.

"Let me play it again," I pleaded. "I'll do better—"

"No." Maestro Claudio shook his head adamantly. "There is nothing I can do to help you." He pointed to my fingers with the tip of his baton. "*These* . . . are not the problem. Come back to see me when you've unmuddled your mind, and then some progress can be made."

Without another word, the maestro huffed into the music department office. With dread in my chest, I stowed my cello in my music locker and hurried into the hallway—and straight into Kiya.

"Sorry," I murmured, and turned away, wanting nothing more than to escape this awkward collision without having to make polite conversation.

"Nadine, hang on," Kiya called after me.

I cringed. I couldn't pretend that I hadn't heard her. I turned to face her, but when she saw my expression, her smile dimmed.

"Whoa, are you okay?" She stepped closer and reached out, as if she wanted to put a hand on my shoulder.

"Sure," I muttered. "Tired, that's all."

She nodded, but her eyes said she wasn't buying that excuse. "That's what I tell people when I'm having an awful day and I don't want them to catch on." My eyes must have betrayed some surprise, because she laughed softly. "What? You don't think I have bad days?"

I shrugged. "You don't seem to. You're always smiling."

She laughed again, then leaned toward me to whisper, "Maybe I'm putting on a good show, but I'm *not* Little Miss Sunshine."

I stared at her. "What do you mean?"

She cocked her head at me. "Well, I left my best friends back in New York. Until a week ago, I didn't know a soul in Woodburn. My dad's having some weird midlife career crisis, and my mom hates it here. She says the cold in Vermont sucks her soul."

I couldn't help my smile. "It *is* cold here." I reluctantly met her gaze. "I didn't realize you were having a tough time," I added. "You're so . . . I don't know . . . put together."

She stuck her hands on her hips and tossed her hair theatrically. "I guess I am," she joked. "I've really been working at it. It's kind of exhausting, smiling all the time, but I figured it was a good way to make new friends. There's something to the whole 'fake it till you make it' idea."

Guilt stung my stomach. For the first time, I considered everything Kiya might be adjusting to. "You must miss New York," I offered up.

She sighed. "So . . . *so* much. The excitement, the bright lights, the skyscrapers . . . the *bagels*!"

I laughed. "Yeah, Woodburn doesn't do bagels. Maple syrup's more our specialty."

She nodded. "Hence the Maple Madness drink at the Snug Mug?"

I felt my spirits flag. "But your dad's getting rid of that."

"Oof." Kiya gave me an apologetic look. "Sore spot. Sorry.

But what exactly do you have against the Snug Mug's changes? Daniel is open to them . . ."

I blushed at the mention of Daniel's name. I was so mad at him—even now—but that didn't change the fact that I also missed him . . . *so much.*

"The thing is, I've heard a few kids at school complaining about the menu change, too," Kiya continued, "but no one will tell me what they think. Like I'm untouchable or something." She rolled her eyes, and I nearly laughed, appreciating the self-deprecation, which made her seem more real and less perfect than usual.

"Do you really care what I think?" I didn't even try to hide the doubt in my voice. "Your family owns the Mug now. You can do whatever you want with it."

She thought about this, then said carefully, "I get that. But my dad has this idea of making the shop sleeker, more city chic. I'm not sure that's what Woodburn is, or what it should be. And . . ." She met my gaze fully now. "Daniel mentioned to me once that there was a story behind how the specialty drinks started, and you were an important part of it. So I figured, if that were true, you could tell me about it."

I swallowed, debating what, if anything, I wanted to tell her. Finally, I settled on the truth, minus some of the more painful details. "It started when Daniel and I were in second grade. He had this idea that if we learned how to make special kinds of coffee, it might bring back something in my life that . . . I'd lost. Marley helped us, and the menu grew from there." I was talking quickly, because I didn't want my own thoughts dwelling on how sweet Daniel had been to do that for me. "It started off as one of the big ideas Daniel is always getting when he wants to make someone happy. You know, like all the surprises he planned for—"

My mouth clamped shut before the word *you* came out, but I wondered if it was too late, because Kiya's eyes widened, and a revelatory light dawned on her face.

"Anyway, that's how it happened," I rushed on.

"Thanks," Kiya said softly. "For telling me what happened. I didn't realize how important . . ." She paused, seeming to debate her next words. ". . . how important the menu was to you." She nodded. "And to everyone in Woodburn."

I shrugged. "It doesn't matter. Your dad's made up his mind, so . . ."

Kiya's phone buzzed with a text then, and she said, "I've gotta go." She started to walk away, then paused, turning back. "I'm glad we talked, Nadine. I hope, once you get to know me more, we can become better friends." She smiled and waved, leaving me standing in the hallway. Despite how much I'd wanted to dislike her, I admired her candor and friendliness, especially in the face of my own standoffishness.

Maybe I hadn't been fair to her. Maybe my opinion of her was as misguided and muddled as so much else in my life.

Dazedly, I walked to my locker. I was half worried and half hoping I'd discover Daniel waiting for me, a sorrowful puppy-dog look on his face. Or maybe Elle and Brandon were there, ready to launch into a long list of the many reasons why I should forgive Daniel so that our circle of friends could survive unscathed. When I found the hallway in front of my locker empty, I guessed, with a mix of relief and disappointment, they'd all decided that the best MO was to let me have some time to process everything on my own.

That was until I opened my locker and hundreds of colorful paper music notes tumbled out. I picked up a handful of notes and read the *I'm sorry* scrawled in Daniel's handwriting across each one.

Ugh. I sank against the lockers just as Elle texted me.

Did you get them? her text read.

I closed my eyes. Of course, Daniel was probably texting Elle or Brandon every few seconds wanting to know if I'd shown any signs of forgiving him yet. Part of me was softened by Daniel's thoughtful gesture. But I couldn't deal with any of it. Not after Maestro Claudio had basically spelled out audition doom for me.

My audition was in three days, and if I didn't pull myself together, I was going to blow my chance at Interlochen camp.

I scooped the notes into my arms and tossed them into the near-est trash can. Next, I turned off my cell phone. I couldn't afford any distractions. I needed to get a grip on my mind and find my musical mojo again, and I was going to have to do it alone.

Four hours later, I hurried back to the music room. I'd managed to avoid my friends for the first half of the day. Now, I planned to spend my lunch period doing battle with my bow until I broke through my burnout.

I was almost to the music room door when Daniel rounded the corner, and my stomach dipped three octaves from my throat to my toes.

"Nadi." He waved to me. "Hold up! Please!" His expression was scared but hopeful, and it pained me to look at it.

My heart tugged at me, asking me to stop, to give Daniel a chance. But my mind could only think of the countdown to the audition, and how every second I spent between now and then *not* practicing was one more second lost.

"I can't," I whispered, and spun away to avoid seeing the hurt on his face. I stepped into the music room and shut the door, leaning against it and fervently hoping he wouldn't follow me inside.

He didn't. Silence swallowed me, and I sank onto the nearest chair. I unpacked my cello, telling myself that this time I'd draw the music from my instrument the way I used to. But each time my bow touched the strings, Daniel's face loomed before my eyes, and the cello screeched instead of sang.

I tried and failed, tried and failed, until panic had my heart racing and my hands were too slick to play at all. There was nothing to be done. I couldn't play. The notes were lost to me, the music gone. Slowly, I laid my bow across the music stand and turned on my phone.

I looked up the Interlochen summer camp admissions number and dialed. Every ring on the line was an alarm blaring. *Failure, failure, failure.* At last, someone answered, and I offered up my name.

"Ms. Durand." The assistant's voice was cursory. "Our

scheduling system shows that your appointment with the camp admissions officer is at eleven a.m. this Thursday in our satellite audition location in Burlington. How can I help you?"

"Yes." I swallowed and dragged the words up into my throat, feeling their burn. "I'm canceling my audition."

For the rest of the school day, minutes turned into eternities as I waded through my classes, my head and heart aching. I'd shut the door on my chance with Interlochen *and* on Daniel. Everything—from the hallway chatter about the upcoming Fall Formal to the test I took (and likely barely passed) in math— disappeared in my fog of gloom.

After the last bell rang, I dragged myself and my cello through the school's doors and into the cold afternoon air. It was only when I heard the gasps and excited buzz of my classmates that I snapped out of my haze long enough to notice what was happening. Crowds of students were lingering on the school's lawn, necks craned back, eyes raised toward the sky.

I followed everyone's gazes to the school's rooftop, and my

head spun at the sight of Daniel standing at the roof's edge. He was hoisting an enormous net over the side of the building, grinning at the kids below, as if this were his finest moment.

"What's he doing?" one girl asked.

"Getting suspended," quipped a boy nearby.

Just then, Kiya and Georgette walked out of the school. At the very same moment, Daniel opened the net overhead to release hundreds of mint-green balloons into the air. They drifted to the ground, cascading over Kiya, who was laughing in delight and surprise.

"They have something written on them," Georgette said, picking one up. She handed it to Kiya. "They're for you."

"What?" Kiya asked, then turned one of the balloons over in her hands and read aloud, "'Kiya, will you go to Fall Formal with me? From, Your Secret Admirer.'"

My chest clenched. He'd done it. Daniel had followed through with his plan, despite the fact that Kiya had been into Graham only a few days ago. He was dauntless in his never-ending optimism, even now, in the face of possible humiliation. He was always putting himself out there, making himself vulnerable.

It was something I'd never been good at. Something I'd always admired about him. But right now, it was a quality I wished he didn't possess. Because right now, as I watched him profess his feelings for this girl, my heart felt like it was cleaving in two.

She'll say no, I told myself, and I watched Kiya for the signs I hoped for—disdain, irritation, aloofness. On her face, though, all I saw was an unexpected joy.

Kiya blushed and, with bafflement, glanced up at Daniel waving from the rooftop.

"Omigod." She laughed softly, shaking her head. "It was Daniel all along?" She looked at Georgette for affirmation, but Georgette only shrugged to show she didn't have a clue about any of it.

Kiya looked back at Daniel, who cupped his hands around his mouth to holler down to her, "Yes or no?"

She laughed, then shrugged, and I saw it, plain as day, on her face. Regardless of whether or not she was in like with Daniel, in this moment, she was charmed by what he'd done for her. Still blushing, Kiya hollered back, "Yes! I'll go with you!"

Whoops and cheers erupted from the kids on the lawn. Kiya cradled the balloon in her arms and chatted excitedly with Georgette, even as Principal Nyugen appeared on the roof to scold Daniel.

A split second of concern for Daniel flitted through me as I thought that, this time, maybe he'd gone too far. As Daniel talked with the principal, though, Ms. Nyugen's face softened. Because who could punish someone for a harmless, well-intentioned disruption like this?

But then Daniel caught my eye, and something indefinable flitted across his face. Regret, maybe, or resignation? I didn't know, but what I *did* know was that I couldn't stay here another moment. Not with everyone around me talking about how romantic and sweet Daniel's gesture was, or how they wished someone would do something like that for them.

It was too much to bear. I turned away and hurried through

the crowd toward Main Street. I told myself I was crying over Interlochen. I told myself that the dull throbbing in my heart had nothing to do with Daniel and Kiya. Daniel and I weren't friends anymore, so I shouldn't care what he did with his life.

When Elle texted me a few minutes later to say she'd be waiting for me at the Snug Mug, and that we needed to talk about Daniel ASAP, I didn't respond.

I wasn't going to the Snug Mug. I didn't want to see Daniel and Kiya together. I didn't want to see anyone. All I wanted to do was go home.

Chapter Eleven

In homeroom the next day, I gripped the sides of my desk, wondering if I could feign a fever to get out of school. I'd barely slept last night, my turmoil over canceling my Interlochen audition compounded by a vision of Daniel and Kiya slow-dancing at the formal.

Last night, when Dad had asked me if I was okay, I'd deflected his question, begging off of dinner and heading straight upstairs. I hadn't said a single word about canceling my audition. I decided I would tell him on Thursday morning when he was ready to drive me to Burlington for the appointment. By then, it would be far too late for him to do anything to change my cancellation. Besides, I'd never change my mind anyway, no matter what anyone said.

Now my stomach cramped at the thought of Interlochen, and then double-cramped as Kiya and Georgette walked into homeroom gabbing about shopping for Fall Formal dresses.

I sighed, trying to tune them out. It was impossible, though. Kiya was right beside me, and I was torn between *not* wanting to hear and desperately needing to.

"Well, the fashion pickings are slim in Woodburn," Georgette was saying, leaning toward Kiya with her phone held up. "I bought my dress weeks ago. Mom and I drove to Burlington to shop."

Kiya looked admiringly at the dress on Georgette's phone. "It's *gorgeous*. I heard about a place in Rutland. Pret-A-Pretty?"

Georgette nodded. "They have cool stuff, but you'll need to go ASAP, because *everybody* goes there for dresses. If you wait too long, there'll be nothing left." Georgette leaned in closer. "Honestly, I'm kind of surprised you're going with Daniel. I thought you might give Graham another chance."

Kiya wrinkled her nose. "No way. Graham is all Heather's." Then she whispered, "Honestly, it's not that I'm into Daniel."

I straightened in my seat, trying to pick up every one of Kiya's barely audible words.

"He's sweet and everything," she continued, "and I'm so flattered by his secret admirer stuff. But, for me, he's more the brotherly type than boyfriend material."

"Then why go with him at all?" Georgette asked. "You could ask anyone in this school. They'd fall all over each other for a chance to go with you."

"That doesn't mean I want to go with any of them," Kiya said. "I said yes to Daniel because I figured it would be nice, and maybe simpler, to go with a friend."

"Does Daniel know that?" The words popped out of my mouth like rogue speech bubbles in a cartoon strip. I wanted to snatch them back as soon as I'd spoken them. But it was too late. Kiya gave me a sheepish look, as if she'd forgotten that I was sitting next to her and that Daniel and I were best friends. Or, I corrected myself, that we *used* to be best friends.

"No," Kiya said softly. "I didn't think he needed to know right away. I can always tell him after the dance."

"Oh right." I stared at her. "So you get what *you* want, a guy on your arm at the dance, and then you break his heart when it's convenient for you and you're done using him."

Kiya looked stricken. "I—I guess I didn't think of it that way," she stammered.

"Maybe you should." My voice was clipped.

The bell rang, and Kiya and I both jumped at the sound. Ms. Bronski shushed us as the morning announcements started over the school's intercom, but Georgette whispered a few final words to Kiya that I overheard clearly:

"Don't worry about what Nadine said. You're not doing anything wrong."

Still, when I glanced at Kiya, I saw her expression creased in deeper embarrassment.

I squirmed. I was still angry at Daniel, but I didn't want to see him used like a pawn in some flirting game, either. Maybe Kiya would rethink her decision to go with Daniel, but I couldn't count on that. And letting Daniel go to the dance thinking that Kiya liked him when *I* knew the truth? That went beyond my frustration with him. That would be cruel.

When the bell rang, I hurried into the hallway and toward Elle's locker. Somebody needed to break the news to Daniel about Kiya, and the sooner the better.

"Hello, stranger," Elle declared upon seeing me waiting for her at her locker. "You don't answer texts or phone calls. I try to make sure you're okay and you stonewall me. And now I'm supposed to welcome you with open arms?" She mock-glared at me. "By all rights, I should be mad at you."

"Please don't be." My voice must've sounded so miserable that it scared her, because she froze, doing a double take of my pained expression.

"Whoa. You do *not* look good." She offered me a sympathetic smile. "Is this about Daniel and Kiya? Wait. Don't answer that. *Of course* it's about Daniel and Kiya."

"You have to talk to Daniel." My tone was urgent. "Or maybe

Brandon can. Or both of you can." I sucked in a breath, then rushed on. "I overheard Kiya and Georgette talking. Kiya doesn't like Daniel. She just wants a date to the dance. She's using him."

"And?" Elle cocked an eyebrow at me, like this was no surprise at all. "What am I supposed to do about it?"

"Elle!" I threw up my hands. "We can't let him go to the dance with her! She'll break his heart. And I'm not speaking to him, so *you* have to be the one to tell him."

Elle thought for a minute, then shook her head. "Nope. Not going to do it this time."

I gaped at her. "What do you mean? He's walking into a trap and you have to warn him."

"Nadi." She sighed. "Brandon and I have been waiting for you two to come to your senses for months now. It boggles the mind that you can't see what's plain as day to us."

I blinked in confusion. "What are you talking about?"

"Okay . . . I'm going to say it." She took a deep breath and reached for my hands. "It's time for you and Daniel to wake up and smell the latte. You two are perfect for each other. Have been since kindergarten." She smiled into my shocked face. "It's true."

"Wha—?" I stuttered as my pulse thudded. "I don't know wh—"

"You *do* know." She squeezed my hands. "In your heart, you've known all along. You and Daniel can practically read each other's minds. Up until the last couple of weeks, you've been inseparable. And"—she shot me a pointed look—"haven't you ever wondered *why* you've been so upset about the whole Operation Kiya thing? It's not because you hate Kiya. She's annoyingly perfect, but she's not hate material."

"It's because . . ." I racked my brain for the many reasons I had for finding Kiya intolerable. But I only found one: Because Daniel had fallen for her. The realization was a thunderbolt striking my brain, and suddenly everything became clear. All of the weird, inexplicable emotions I'd had over the last few weeks, my annoyance over Operation Kiya, the thrill I had whenever Daniel brushed my hand with his. "Omigod . . ." I sucked in a breath and stared at Elle, whose own face lit up at the dawning of realization on mine.

"Yes." She nodded encouragingly. "You like him."

"I do!" I blurted out, blushing. I couldn't believe I hadn't admitted it to myself before.

I liked Daniel.

"But . . . I can't," I added the next second. "He likes Kiya!" I slumped against the lockers. "And he's my best friend—*was* my best friend."

"Hello?" Elle singsonged. "Best friends make the best boyfriends. For example, me and Brandon." She grinned proudly, as if she were sharing great wisdom. "And, FYI, Daniel *doesn't* like Kiya. He's been starstruck by her, the same as everybody else. He doesn't even know her. Not like he knows you."

"I guess that's true," I admitted. "But we're not even speaking to each other right now!"

"So . . . ?" Her eyes widened as she waited for me to come to the obvious conclusion. I knew it, but couldn't say it, so she finally said, "That's why *you* have to be the one to tell him about Kiya."

"But . . ." Panic constricted my throat. "I have no idea how he'll react."

Elle gave me a knowing look. "For once, all the planning in the world isn't going to guarantee you one hundred percent certainty that things are going to work out. You're the most organized person I know, but you can't schedule a perfect time for love. So, forget about your calendar and all the what-if scenarios and go for it."

"You're right," I muttered, more to myself than to her. Then I glanced at her as she nodded fervently. "You're totally right!"

She beamed, and bowed gleefully. "My job here is done. Thank you very much."

For the first time in days, I found myself smiling. It wasn't a full-blown, life-is-perfect smile. It couldn't be, when I'd blown my chance at Interlochen. It was a smile of uncertainty and fear, but also of possibility. The bell rang, and Elle and I shouldered our bags.

"We have to get to class." Elle hugged me. "You've got this." She headed down the hallway, waving and smiling. "Call me later. I won't say a word until I hear from you."

I nodded, then pulled out my phone, texting Daniel as I walked.

Meet me at the Snug Mug after school, I wrote with trembling fingers. Code Red. We need to talk.

I swallowed down the last sip of my mournfully plain cappuccino and checked my phone again. No text from Daniel yet, and no sign of him, either. I set down the paper cup, my hands trembling.

What if he didn't come? I peered through the open slats of the loft's banister. The afternoon crowd at the Snug Mug was down by half, and I guessed it was because of Mr. Renaud's new menu. While I'd been waiting for Daniel, I'd watched a half dozen regulars wander into the shop and then leave just as quickly. Disappointment and discontented mutterings abounded.

Kiya was behind the counter with her dad. She had glanced my way when I'd walked in, her happy-to-help-you barista smile slipping from her face.

Her guilty look meant that she hadn't told Daniel how she really felt. After my talk with Elle, though, I was actually okay with that.

I wanted to be the one to break it to Daniel, for better or for worse. I was ready. Or—I checked my vibrato pulse and burning cheeks—if I wasn't exactly ready, at least I was getting there.

As soon as that thought crossed my mind, there was Daniel walking in the front door. My heart pounded out allegro sixteenth notes in quick succession. It was as if I were seeing Daniel for the thousandth time and for the first time. There was the wavy black hair, broad shoulders, and sparkling brown eyes. His expression—full of kindness, and a laugh that always seemed to be waiting beneath the surface—was familiar, but it affected me in ways it never had before. I felt myself go a little weak at his handsomeness. It was something I'd never openly acknowledged—or maybe never let myself appreciate—until now.

I expected him to stop at the counter to offer a smitten smile to Kiya, but he climbed the stairs two steps at a time without even glancing her way. I stood, then sat, then stood again, at a loss as to the best position to be in to share the news.

The moment he crossed the stairs' threshold, though, I stopped thinking and rushed toward him, and he did the same.

"I'm so sorry!" we both blurted, and then our arms were wrapped around each other, the way they had been so many other times throughout our lives. I wasn't even sure what I was apologizing for. It might've been for taking so long to realize what I should've seen ages ago—that Daniel was the first and only boy I'd ever fallen for.

My skin prickled as his hands cupped my waist. When I lifted my head from his shoulder, I saw in his eyes a surprise and momentary confusion, as if maybe he'd felt something in our hug, too. My heart pounded. Then he took a step back, his hands slipping away.

"*I'm* the one who needs to apologize," he said. "I should never have gotten involved in the situation between your mom and you. I got carried away." He smiled sheepishly. "Like I always do."

I met his gaze, and nearly lost my train of thought. I'd always thought that Daniel had nice eyes, but now they cast a spell on

me with their welcoming warmth. I mentally shook myself . . .
I had to focus.

"I know you meant well," I said softly. "But being blindsided
wasn't great. *I* wanted to be the one to decide when, or if, I was
ready to see Mom."

He nodded. "I wanted to give you what *I'd* always wanted
to have."

"What do you mean?"

"A chance to see my dad again." His voice was so quiet, I had
to lean toward him to hear it. "I thought it would be great for
you to get to know your mom, in ways that I never got to know
Appa . . ."

I felt my heart squeeze. "Oh, Daniel. I'm sorry. I never thought
about that . . ."

"That's okay." He smiled sadly at me. "You didn't need to
think about it because your mom is still around. She's not gone
forever. I guess I was a little annoyed with you for ignoring her.
It was tough for me to see you being so nonchalant about her, like
you didn't appreciate what you had."

I thought this over. "In some ways, it seems easier to pretend like she's gone forever. Safer. Because if she's already gone . . ." My voice broke. "She can't leave me all over again."

"But your mom's *here* and she wants you in her life. That seems too important to ignore."

I stared at my toes, wanting to argue with that and finding I couldn't.

"Safe isn't always perfect, Nadi. It can make you miss out on things." Daniel ran a hand through his hair. "I actually talked to *my* mom about that this week, too. You know, about how she drowns herself in work so she can pretend Appa never existed at all. That's *her* safety net."

"Wow. What did she say?"

"Well, after a lot of ranting in Kugo, Omma admitted that *maybe* she works too much and can cut back on her hours at the hospital. She also got out some of the old photo albums. She's never going to be the huggy, mushy-mom type, and she still has a hard time talking about Appa, but"—he grinned—"it's progress."

"That's great." I smiled, feeling relieved for him. "And I understand why you did what you did with me and my mom. You went overboard, but . . . I get it."

"So we're okay?" He stepped closer, peering into my eyes. "I need to make sure, because if anything ever came between us . . . if I lost our friendship . . ." His voice faltered.

"You won't." A warm energy hummed in the small space between us, and my heart strummed a happy arpeggio. "I promise."

Daniel wiped his brow theatrically. "Phew! Because I'm going to need your help with Fall Formal. I mean, what do you wear on a date with a goddess—"

"Daniel," I interrupted, taking a step back, "about the formal and Kiya." My stomach knotted with dread. The two of us had just gotten on good terms again, and now I was potentially about to ruin it all with what I had to tell him. I drew a deep breath. "I heard Kiya talking to Georgette earlier today." I swallowed thickly. "Kiya doesn't like you. Not in that way. She only agreed to go to the dance with you so that she'd have a date."

Daniel's eyes widened. "No." He shook his head. "She loved the Operation Kiya surprises. And she said yes right away . . ."

"I know you don't want it to be true," I said gently. "Believe me, I wish we weren't even having the conversation right now. But . . . at least talk to Kiya and find out for yourself."

He was still shaking his head, but there was a shift in his expression, as if, somewhere deep down inside, he already sensed that what I told him was right.

"You could still go with her," I suggested, even though my heart panged at the idea. "If she really means that much to you."

"And compromise my integrity?" His tone was reaching toward joking but falling short. "Nah. A guy has to have standards. But, man, this is embarrassing. I've been a total goner, haven't I?"

"It's understandable," I conceded. "She's pretty perfect."

He tilted his head at me. "Maybe not like I thought." He sighed. "I guess my romantic gestures could only do so much."

I laughed softly. "Hey . . ." I nudged his arm with mine. "You're going to find a girl who likes you, romantic gestures and all." *Maybe like me*, I thought hopefully.

He nodded reluctantly, then brightened. "So maybe I'm not going to Fall Formal after all . . ." He shrugged. "I'll survive, as long as you can at least tell me that I can still go with you to your Interlochen audition Thursday."

My insides shriveled, and I dropped my eyes. I'd promised Daniel ages ago that he could come along for moral support. "About that . . ." My voice was barely a whisper. "I'm not going."

"What?" Daniel hollered, and for a moment the customers in the shop below stilled.

I shushed him. "I canceled my audition, but I haven't told anyone else."

Daniel frowned. "Why would you do that? What were you thinking?"

"I'm not even close to ready. I haven't been able to practice since . . ." *Since you fell for Kiya*, I realized. But I couldn't admit that, so instead said, "Since the whole thing happened with Mom. My playing sounds like croaking frogs. It's awful. And I haven't finished my composition piece—"

"So finish it." Daniel's words were matter-of-fact, like there was no other option. "You fix the problem, and you go to the audition—"

"I'll never make it in. I don't have enough time to fix everything. Besides . . ." I straightened my shoulders even as my spirit drooped. "I've made up my mind."

"Nadi." His expression was pleading. "You've wanted this for so long."

"Please," I whispered as my eyes filled with tears. "Let it go."

He opened his mouth like he wanted to argue more, then stopped himself. Instead, he stepped toward me, his arms outstretched for a hug.

I longed to feel his arms around me again, but froze, backing away. He still had things to work out with Kiya. Maybe he needed time to get over her. Plus, even if *my* feelings for him had grown into something new, *his* might not have changed at all. If I let myself get close to him now, and he caught on to my feelings for him and freaked, I wasn't sure I'd ever recover.

"I've got to go," I choked out as my tears threatened to spill over.

"Wait," he started. "Can I come over for dinner tonight? We can talk about it—"

I shook my head. "I'll see you tomorrow at school, okay?" I tried to muster a smile, but it crumpled at the edges. "I'll be fine."

I felt his eyes on me as I ran down the stairs and out the shop's door. No matter how much he might want to, this was one problem Daniel couldn't magic away with balloons or flowers. No one could fix this, and the sooner I came to terms with that, the better.

Chapter Twelve

"Nadi!" Dad's voice called from the family room. "I've got to go. You'll get yourself off to school okay?"

I was still in bed, in pajamas, not even close to being ready for school. Dad didn't know that, though. If I could pull a Ferris Bueller—this *one* time—Dad would leave without ever figuring out that I had no intention of going to school today. I reached down deep and rallied my cheeriest voice. "No problem! I'll see you later."

I'd spent all of last night in my room, not even coming downstairs to eat. My talk with Daniel stuck like syrup to every thought I had. It wasn't just the reaction he'd had to my news about Interlochen, either. It was what he'd said about Mom.

Your mom's here and she wants you in her life, he'd said. *That seems too important to ignore.*

Those words echoed in my mind until they blocked everything else out. Everything, that is, except the audition I was missing in just over twenty-four hours.

"I'm nervous about the audition, that's all" was what I told Dad when I'd said I wasn't hungry. It didn't really matter what excuse I offered, because since our fight, Dad and I had barely exchanged more than a sentence or two. Dad had been even more remote than usual, making phone calls in his room with the door closed and spending hours on his laptop. And he was acting strange, snapping his laptop shut the second I walked into the room.

"I'll see you this afternoon, then." Dad's voice sounded uncertain now. "Remember I'm not in Woodburn today. I'm doing fieldwork outside of Rutland. Call my cell if you need me."

"Sounds good!" The fact that Dad wasn't in town today only worked in my favor. The farther away he was, the smaller the chance he'd find out my plan.

I waited for the sound of the front door closing. As soon as I heard it, I threw off my covers and reached for my phone. My heart was racing.

I stared at the number on the screen. Once I called, there'd be no turning back. I took a do-or-die breath and hit call. My phone didn't even make it through the first ring before a nervous but familiar voice picked up.

"Nadi?" Mom's tone was happy and terrified all at once. "Is it you?"

I gripped the phone so tightly that my fingertips went numb. "It's me. I was wondering . . . I mean, if you're not too busy . . ." My voice was warbling, and I fought to steady it. "I'd like to see you," I blurted at last. "I was thinking . . . today would be good?"

"Oh, Nadi." Mom's voice broke, and I didn't know if it was with relief or regret. Was she about to tell me that she *was* too busy? Or that she'd decided Boston was too boring a place to settle down? Or that she was leaving for Timbuktu—or wherever—in a few minutes? "I'd love to see you. But . . . don't you have school today?"

I braced myself for the words I was about to say next. They were words that went against every ounce of my organized, rule-following self. "Actually, I was wondering if you could call me in sick."

"I don't know," she said slowly. "I'm not sure your dad would be too happy about that, but . . . maybe give me some background?"

I blew out a breath. Where to even begin? "I messed up something that was really important to me. Dad doesn't know about it yet. And . . ." My voice warbled again, this time from the rush of tears flooding down my face. "I don't ever lie to him. About anything." I sniffed into the phone, choking on a sob. "I'm sad. I'm just really sad, and—"

"I'm already in my car," Mom interrupted. In the background, I heard an engine starting. "Hang tight. It's going to be a couple of hours, but I'll be there as soon as I can."

*　　*　　*

When the doorbell finally rang, I froze, thinking that one of two things was about to happen. One, I was going to be sick. Two, I was going to open the front door to find my mom on the other side of it. I waited for a solid ten seconds, but then my nausea passed, and I was able to walk to the door and open it.

I wasn't shocked by the sight of Mom's face like I'd been last time at the Snug Mug. But I was still so nervous that my hand shook when I lifted it to give Mom a wave.

She looked as jumpy as I felt. "I brought some donut holes." She held out a brown paper bag and a tray holding two coffees. "The chocolate glazed used to be your favorites."

"They still are," I said in surprise. "You . . . remember that?"

"I left," she said quietly, "but I didn't forget." Silence fell between us for a moment, and then she cleared her throat, nodding to the coffee tray in her hand. "I think you like pumpkin spice lattes but when I stopped at the Snug Mug they didn't have them on the menu anymore, so I got us cappuccinos . . ." Her voice trailed off, and her shoulders tensed with awkwardness. "I shouldn't have brought them. That was silly. I know that day I met you there was a mistake—"

"No, it's okay." I took the coffees from her and opened the door wider so that she could come inside. "I haven't wanted to eat much, but donut holes actually sound good."

"Do they?" The relief in her voice was palpable. "I'm glad." She stepped over the threshold and shrugged out of her coat. Then she followed me into the family room, the two of us moving gingerly around each other in an awkward dance. Finally, we settled on different ends of the couch. Not too close to each other, but we had to start somewhere.

I nibbled at one of the donut holes while Mom took a hefty swig of her coffee.

"We have a lot to talk about, I know," Mom said. "But maybe you want to start with why you look like you've been crying for hours?"

I hesitated, studying her face. I recognized remnants of the mom from my childhood, but her presence in our family room seemed too strange to be real.

"I'm not even sure why I called you," I admitted. "I wanted

to talk to somebody, so . . ." I shrugged, at a loss as to how to explain the impulse I'd had earlier. But—if I was totally honest with myself—this was the first time in six years I'd even been able to reach my mom in an emergency. Having her pick up the phone when I'd dialed had felt . . . good. Reassuring. I sank my head into my hands. "This is so confusing! I don't even know what I'm supposed to say, or even think."

Silence stretched between us, and I felt the couch cushions rise and then fall as Mom moved to sit beside me. With a careful slowness, as if she wanted to gauge my reaction, she reached for my hands and drew them away from my face.

"Maybe we forget 'supposed tos,'" she said softly. "There's no set of rules for this." She offered me a tentative smile. "Tell me what feels right to tell me. Ask me anything. Yell, cry, scream. Whatever you need to do. I'm here."

I met her gaze, and even as I felt all the emotions building inside me—the anger at her for leaving, the blame I wanted to place on her, the pain of missing her all those years—they weren't what I needed to talk about first.

I took a deep breath. "Okay, so you know I play the cello . . ." She nodded encouragingly. "And I had an audition for Interlochen's camp scheduled for tomorrow, but . . ."

I kept on, the words pouring out of me more effortlessly than I ever would've imagined. I kept talking, and Mom kept listening. At some point, I started to understand why I'd been compelled to call her. It was comforting to talk to someone who didn't know me well enough to offer me instant advice, or who would presume to tell me what was best, or what I should do.

Daniel had been so quick to try to convince me I was making a mistake, and Dad . . . What *would* Dad say when he found out? Probably nothing. Like he always did.

Mom listened openly and without judgment. She asked questions, but if I couldn't or didn't want to answer, she yielded without pushing. It was such a relief that by the time I'd talked myself out, I'd finished off the bag of donut holes and was sagging into the couch.

"You know, it's funny, what a careful planner you are," Mom said at last, running her finger in a circle around her coffee cup lid. "You got that from your father. Sometimes I think the only spontaneous thing he ever did was marry me." She smiled at the memory like it was a happy one, and I was glad. "Oh, and having you." She nodded toward Dad's bedroom. "Did he tell you that you were born in that bedroom?"

I shook my head. "I *was*? Dad never told me! He's not exactly a super talker."

"No, he always was on the quiet side." She laughed softly. "Anyway, you were born two weeks early in that back room. We didn't have time to get to the hospital. I told your father you already had an adventurous spirit, since you couldn't wait another minute to see the world."

I smiled wryly. "But I don't have that spirit," I said. "I overthink everything. And I hate change. It terrifies me."

"Same with your dad," Mom said. "He was scared of being a parent. But as soon as you were born, it was suddenly like he knew that all he had to do in life was make sure he kept you safe. We were practically kids ourselves, but in that instant, he grew up. Just like that." Her voice dropped into sadness. "He wasn't the one who ran. That was me. In the end, *I* was the one too scared to stay."

My anger rose to the surface then. "Scared of me?"

"The responsibility of you. Of knowing how easily I could mess everything up, or mess *you* up." Her voice wavered, and she dabbed at her eyes. "It wasn't bravery that made me leave. I told your dad I wanted adventure, but really, I was terrified of the biggest adventure of all." She met my gaze, tears in her eyes. "Raising you."

I battled back my own tears, not willing to show her how much her words hurt.

"I knew I was making mistakes as a young mom," she said, "but what scared me the most was the mistakes I might be making with you that I *didn't* know about yet. There were so many things that could go wrong, and I was responsible for your whole life . . ." Her voice trailed off. "My fear robbed me of you, and I'll regret that forever. What I wish for you"—she met my gaze—"is that you don't let fear control you, or leave you with regret for all the things you might've done but didn't. What a loss that would be, for you . . . and the world." There was glimmer of feistiness in her eyes, the same feistiness that had carried her around the globe.

I clenched my hands together, frowning. "I've hated you for leaving."

Her mouth crumpled, but she nodded. "That's fair. Nothing I could ever say will make up for the years I've missed. All I'm hoping is for a chance to get to know you again. I'll be as big or as little a part of your life as you'd like." Her voice broke, and for a few minutes, she couldn't speak. Then, at last, she added in a whisper, "I'd just like to be a part. Any part."

My heart skipped with fear, doubt, and hope. "I'm not sure what I can give you," I said. "I don't trust you." I swallowed, then added, "Yet."

"I don't blame you." She wiped her eyes again.

Then it was my turn to cautiously reach out and slowly take her hand. "But I'll try."

She squeezed my hand, smiling. "I'll try, too."

I sighed, suddenly feeling exhausted to the bone. I hadn't slept well the past few nights. It had only been a couple hours since Mom had arrived, but there was a universe of change between then and now. I'd opened a door to her, and no matter how terrifying the prospect of it was, I wanted it to stay open. But I also needed time to process.

"This is a lot." My voice was quiet. "But . . . I think it's good."

Mom's eyes brightened. "Me, too," she whispered. Then, as if she'd picked up on my fatigue, or maybe my need to be alone for a while, she stood. "Your dad's probably going to be home soon, so I think I should go." She paused, then added, "I *did* call him earlier to tell him I was on my way over. You might not like that I did that, but in order for this to work, we have to start off on the right foot. Honesty is an absolute nonnegotiable." I nodded, somewhat grudgingly, but then she added, "And he's not angry with you about missing school. He said he was sure it was a one-time thing."

"It was." Guilt over missing school had zapped me countless times today. I still wasn't cut out for breaking the rules, but since

I hadn't brought on Armageddon, I guessed it was okay . . . just this once.

I followed Mom to the entryway, and we hovered by the door, both of us stalling.

"Well," Mom said, "I'm not sure how much of a help I was. Six years makes for a steep learning curve." She smiled at me. "But I'm so glad you called."

"Me, too," I said, and meant it. "And you did help."

She hesitated, her hand on the door. There was a yearning in her eyes, and I guessed that she wanted to hug me. She was letting me take the lead, but I wasn't sure what I wanted or was ready for, either.

"All right, well . . ." She opened the door.

"Mom, wait." I wrapped my arms around her, at first tentatively, and then more snugly. She enveloped me in the warmth of her own arms. "I hope we'll talk again soon."

"Anytime," Mom whispered, giving me a squeeze. I let go first, and she stepped through the door.

I waved as her car pulled out of the driveway. Then I collapsed back on the couch, feeling drained but relieved and unconscionably happy.

I burrowed beneath a blanket, unable to keep my eyes open a second longer. My insides had been wound so tight for so long, and now the coil gave way, unspooling. As I fell into a deep, restful sleep, Mom's words fluttered through my drifting thoughts: *Don't let fear control you.*

I won't, came my mind's far-off answer.

"Nadi," a familiar voice was whispering, and there was a gentle hand resting on my shoulder. "Nadi, hon. It's time to wake up."

"Dad?" I asked, pulling myself from the depths of my dreamless sleep. I sat up slowly, disoriented for a minute by the dimly lit family room and crackling fire in the potbellied stove. Dad was perched on the arm of the sofa, looking down at me with a tender smile—a smile I hadn't seen on his face in I couldn't remember how long. "Wha—what time is it?" I glanced out the darkened window.

"Not too late," he said. "Around six. You still have plenty of time."

"Plenty of time to do what?" I sat up straighter, for the first time noticing the paper bag Dad was holding in his lap, and the purposeful expression on his face.

"To get ready for your audition tomorrow." His tone was steady and straightforward, and it made my stomach sink.

"Dad . . ." I shook my head. "I thought Mom might've told you already, but . . . I canceled the audition. I'm not going tomorrow."

"Your mom didn't tell me. Daniel did."

My pulse triple-timed at hearing Daniel's name. "What?"

Dad nodded. "He texted me yesterday, right after you left the Snug Mug."

"But . . ." I tried to piece together this information. "You didn't say anything. You knew last night, and—"

"I figured that if I brought it up, you'd only make it impossible for me to do what I knew I had to do."

My brow crinkled in confusion. "What did you do?"

"I called Interlochen, and your audition is back on for tomorrow." He gave my knee a single, definitive pat. "So that's that."

I opened my mouth, prepared for panicked words of refusal to fly out. None came. I waited for my heartbeat to race full throttle into terror, for alarm bells of anxiety to scream in my head. Nothing. What I felt, instead, was an ember ignite inside me, in the very spot where my fear had lodged for so long. My body had already decided what my mind hadn't caught on to yet—that I still wanted to audition. That, no matter how ill-prepared I was, I needed to try.

I stared at Dad, and saw in his eyes a mirror of my resolve. "How . . . how did you know I'd still want to?"

"I didn't." He leaned toward me. "But you're not a quitter, so I thought my chances were pretty good." He smiled again, then took a deep breath. "You've been angry with me, and I'm sorry. I'm not the world's best conversationalist. Never have been." He swept a hand through his hair. "It used to bug your mom, too. It was one of the things we fought about, that I wasn't good at 'emoting.'" He gave a small laugh at the word.

"It's the way you are," I conceded, "but . . . I get lonely sometimes."

He moved to sit beside me on the couch. "I'm so sorry about that, hon. You've made it too easy on me, being as grown-up as you are. You were always like that, even as a little kid." He gave me an awkward side hug. It didn't last long, but I felt its warmth, all the same. "Heck, you even organized your carpools in elementary school, remember? I started thinking that there wasn't much left for me to do. You handled everything so well on your own."

"I always needed you, Dad." I took his hand. "I still do."

He smiled at me. "Thanks for the reminder."

I rested my head on his shoulder, and the two of us sat there for a long minute in comfortable silence.

"I've been thinking we should shake things up in the kitchen," Dad said then. "I'm sick of chili, aren't you?"

I laughed. "Dad, I've been sick of it for the last two years."

He reached into the paper shopping bag in his lap and pulled out a book called *How to Cook Everything*. "I thought we could work our way through this cookbook together. And I'll keep learning recipes while you're at Interlochen. By the time you come home at the end of summer, I'll be able to cook . . . well, anything." He seemed to consider what he'd just said, then added, "Except for lima beans. I've never liked them much."

I laughed. "Me, neither."

"You have no idea how much I'm going to miss you when you're gone," Dad said.

"You're assuming I'm going to get accepted," I replied.

"You will," he said simply, then stood up. "Oh, and that reminds me. There's one other important thing I picked up while I was shopping today." He held up a finger. "Wait right here."

He disappeared into his bedroom and returned a minute later, holding a brand-new, beautiful Ivan Dunov cello.

"Omigod." I ran my hands over the cello's polished surface. It was absolutely stunning. "Wait, Dad!" I cried, glancing up at him in shock. "Is this . . . Is it . . ."

"It's all yours." Dad grinned proudly. "I drove to Rutland to pick it up today. I had to have it special ordered. I've been saving for it since your first concert years ago. I'm only sorry it's taken me so long to be able to give it to you."

I threw my arms around his neck and kissed his cheek. When I pulled away, his face was bright red. "Dad, this is incredible. I love it." My eyes welled. "Thank you."

He cleared his throat. "You better get practicing. You have an audition to get ready for, and I have to unpack some groceries." As he turned toward the kitchen, the doorbell rang. "Well, now, I wonder who that could be?" He shot me a smile, then added a mysterious, "Nadi, get the door while I unload the bags?"

I gave him a questioning glance, but opened the door to find Daniel on the other side, holding a Snug Mug takeout bag. I tried not to blush at the sight of him.

He didn't even wait for me to say anything, but blew past me into the entryway, nodding at my dad, as if the two of them had this plotted out all along.

"I'm here for the long haul," Daniel said matter-of-factly. "I'm not leaving until your composition piece is finished and you're audition-ready." He reached into the Snug Mug bag and set down two takeout containers overflowing with s'mores waffles. "I brought these, and your dad picked up all the ingredients for Pumpkin Spice Supremes."

I glanced into the kitchen to see Dad holding up a jar of pumpkin puree in one hand and a bag of espresso beans in the other.

I shook my head, laughing. "You two did not!"

"Oh, we absolutely did!" Daniel said. He pumped his fist in the air. "Team Nadi right here!"

I laughed, and even Dad chuckled from the kitchen.

"So." Daniel planted his hands on the coffee table like a no-nonsense detective questioning a suspect. "Are you going to get to work or what?"

I straightened my shoulders and nodded. "Bring on the pumpkin spice lattes and the sixteenth-note triplet runs."

Daniel blinked. "The lattes I can do. The . . . whatever you just said about triplet marathons . . . is all you."

I gave him a thumbs-up, but my heart tugged to follow him as he headed into the kitchen. I was beyond glad that he was here, but there were so many questions I wanted to ask him. Had he talked to Kiya about the dance? What had she said? What if he'd decided to go to the dance with her anyway, even after everything?

I shook off the questions. Now wasn't the time. If I was going to give the audition my all, I had to start right now.

I dragged my practicing chair into the center of the room, set up my music stand, and then carefully took the amazingly beautiful Ivan Dunov cello into my hands. After a few tentative warm-ups, I lifted my bow, closed my eyes, and dove headlong into my music.

Daniel leaned back against the pillows, his hands cocked beneath his head, listening as I drew my bow across the strings one last time. My eyes were trained on his face, watching and waiting anxiously for his reaction.

My arms ached, my fingertips were stinging and partly numb, and even my calluses had calluses. The coffee table was strewn with waffle crumbs and empty coffee cups, water glasses and chocolate wrappers (when the waffles had run out, we'd resorted to Hershey's Kisses for fuel). Composition sheets—those I'd rejected with their crossed-out measures and eraser smudges—littered the couch and floor. I had no idea what time it was, but when I'd last checked, my phone screen had read a quarter past two in the morning. Dad had gone to bed an hour ago, but Daniel and I had pushed onward. Finally, painstakingly, I'd finished my composition, and my audition piece was as smooth, polished, and good as it was going to get.

I lifted my bow from the strings and held my breath as the music faded. When Daniel didn't move a muscle, I started to worry he'd fallen asleep and missed the performance completely. "Daniel?" I whispered, setting down my cello to try to stretch the soreness from my arms. "Are you still awake?"

I could hardly blame him if he wasn't. He'd put in hours with me, and we were beyond exhausted.

Slowly, he opened his eyes and smiled. "That . . . was phenomenal. You're ready."

"Ooooh . . . thank God." I collapsed onto the floor, so grateful to be lying down at last that I didn't even care about the papers crinkling beneath me. "If you'd told me it wasn't working. *Again . . .*" I tried to raise my head to glare at him but couldn't. "I might've spurned you forever."

"You wouldn't have." He grinned and slipped to the floor beside me. "You love me too much for that. Admit it."

"I . . ." My pulse stuttered out its own reply. I didn't want tonight to end on an awkward note, so I reluctantly fought the urge to tell him what my heart longed to say. "Hey." I lifted my head then, realizing, with surprise, that he hadn't brought Kiya up all night. "You never told me what happened with Kiya. Did you talk to her?"

He groaned. "I'm not sure my sleep-deprived brain cells can cope with the rehash, but I'll try." He grabbed a pillow from the couch for himself and lay back down. "Long story short: I talked to her and . . . you were right." He stared up at the ceiling. "She basically said she only liked me as a friend. But she was nice about it." He sighed. "We *could* still go to the dance as friends."

"Oh . . ." My heart plummeted. "Right."

He studied my face for a long moment that made my pulse quicken. "But we're not," he said slowly. "Going to go together."

"Oh!" I exclaimed, then could've kicked myself a second later for how happy my voice sounded. "Why not?"

He swiveled onto his side to face me. "Because I deserve better than to be somebody's second choice." His tone was certain, his eyes locked on mine.

"You do," I whispered. "I'm sorry, though. I know you're disappointed." Yet as I searched his face for signs of heartache, I saw a surprisingly calm acceptance.

He gave me a sleepy smile. "You're not *that* sorry."

I laughed through a big yawn. "True."

"You know, it's funny . . . I'm not as upset as I thought I'd be." He shrugged. "The fact is, I don't really know her that well. It was like I was chasing after this beautiful mirage in the distance, but it wasn't the real deal. Now I know better." He met my gaze. "Next time, my heart's holding out for the one-of-a-kind oasis."

"Oasis." I smiled tiredly. "Daniel. You have impossible standards." My eyes were starting to close against my will, and I struggled to keep them open. I glanced at Daniel, whose eyes were fluttering closed, too.

"Not impossible." He yawned and mumbled something that I thought sounded like, "I have you . . ."

"Daniel . . ." I whispered. I tried to stay awake long enough to tell him that I was glad, *more* than glad, that he'd realized Kiya wasn't right for him. Long enough to confess what was in my own heart. But sleep was the symphony I couldn't ignore, and before I could say more, I was drifting into its melody, comforted by the fact that Daniel was near, only an arm's length away.

Chapter Thirteen

I was pulled from sleep by the sound of our coffee maker gurgling to life with a hiss of steam. I groggily opened my eyes and found myself staring into Daniel's sleeping face, right near mine. I registered that we were still on the family room floor, nestled in the piles of composition papers left over from last night's musical blitzkrieg. Somehow, our hands had found each other during the night, because right now, my hands were clasped snugly and warmly in Daniel's.

My heart thrummed happily in my chest, and I stayed as

still as possible, wanting to linger near him. I couldn't take my eyes off his lips. I wondered what they would feel like to kiss.

He made a quiet stirring sound, and a lock of his hair slipped over his forehead. Before I even realized what I was doing, I slid my hand from his to brush the hair back from his face. As my fingertips grazed his temple, his eyes opened.

"Nadi," he whispered in a tone that made me love the way he said my name. My hand froze, and I wondered if he'd jump up, startled by our close proximity.

But his eyes were dream-steeped, and instead, he smiled slowly. I still wasn't sure if he was fully awake or half asleep as his head moved toward mine, and then my eyes closed, and—

"Rise and shine, kiddos." Dad's voice made my eyes spring open. Blushing wildly, I scooted away from Daniel, banging my head against the coffee table in the process. Daniel quickly sat up, a mixture of confusion and embarrassment on his face. Dad glanced over at us, taking in the mess of papers and our make-shift beds on the floor. I snuck a side glance at Daniel, and we both smiled sheepishly. "Better get a move on," Dad said. "I'm making coffee and breakfast sandwiches to take with us in the car. We've got to hit the road in fifteen."

"Omigod!" I cried, forgetting the awkwardness of the last thirty seconds. "I've got to get ready."

I lunged for the loft stairs while Daniel started scooping up some of the empty mugs and papers.

"I'll clean up down here and make you a Pumpkin Spice Supreme to go," he called after me.

"Thank you," I said gratefully, and flew upstairs, adrenaline transforming my tiredness into frenetic energy.

Fifteen minutes later, we were pulling out of the driveway with Burlington plugged into Waze and a paper cup of Daniel's Pumpkin Spice Supreme in my hands, warming me and fueling me with determination.

All too soon, we were waiting in the hallway of the music building at the University of Vermont. The scene was chaotic; each musician waiting to audition tuned and retuned their instrument, or practiced that last measure with the tricky fingering. Dad paced, while Daniel stood by my side, giving me a smile that reminded me he had confidence in me, no matter what. I hugged my new cello to my chest, willing the perspiration slicking my fingertips to dry before the audition coordinator called my name.

I sucked in a breath and caught Daniel studying my face. "What?" I asked.

He shook his head, his smile never wavering. "I get that you might be hyperventilating on the inside, but on the outside . . ." He gave me two thumbs up. "Calm, cool, collected—"

"About to pass out," I offered, to which he laughed.

"You always get this fierce expression before you perform. Like you're *that* good, and you know it."

"Ha ha." I rolled my eyes. "I *don't* know it."

He reached for my hand, and my breath caught. "Your fingers do."

For a second, as he held my hand in his, I wondered if he were about to raise it to his lips.

"Nadine Durand." My heart spasmed as I turned to see the

audition coordinator peering over her iPad at the faces around the room.

"I'm Nadine." I glanced back at Dad and Daniel.

"You got this," Dad said, giving me a quick hug, while Daniel gave my hand one final squeeze.

"Thank you," I told them both. I couldn't have done this without them.

I forced my feet to move. One step, then two, then a dozen, past the other waiting auditioners and into the quiet room beyond. A panel of three admissions personnel sat solemnly at a long table. I eased onto the empty chair, my cello beside me, the loyal, constant friend it was.

"Ms. Durand." The spectacled man in the middle of the table gave me a brief but kind smile. "The title of the original composition you'll be performing for us today, if you please."

"Oh." My resolve faltered in the face of this question. Since I'd only finished the piece last night, I hadn't yet named it. Panic rose in me, then stilled. I had the name. I'd known it all along. "'Daniel's Song.'" My voice was even and smooth.

The man jotted it down on his notepad. "You may begin when you're ready."

"Daniel's Song." I smiled. It was perfect for the piece that I'd written with Daniel by my side. It was a piece that sang of our friendship, of the laughter and Fallfests and coffees we'd shared together through the years. It was a piece I could play by heart, without nervousness, because it was a piece that came *from* my heart. I rested my cello's neck tenderly against my shoulder, lifted my bow, and played.

"Nadi? Daniel? We're here."

At the sound of Dad's voice, I opened my eyes to find my head resting on Daniel's shoulder. We were in the back seat of the car, and had just pulled into the driveway of Daniel's house. Daniel stirred, too, and sat up, pushing his hair out of his eyes.

"You two have been out for the last hour," Dad said. Then to Daniel, he added, "Better get yourself to bed early tonight. It's been a long day."

Daniel glanced at me with a grin. "Yep. But a good one."

I grinned back. The second I'd left the audition room, Dad and Daniel had been waiting to envelop me in a double hug.

"You nailed it." Daniel had beamed at me.

"You don't know that—"

"It's you, Nadi." He nodded confidently. "I know."

I wouldn't find out whether I'd gotten accepted to Interlochen camp for at least another month, but I had a good feeling about it. "Daniel's Song" had flowed flawlessly from my cello. As I'd played, everything and everyone else in the room had faded away, until it was just me and the music. I didn't know what the admissions panel would decide, but I'd given them the best performance of my life so far. That was all I could ask for.

Now I followed Daniel out of the car, calling to Dad over my shoulder, "Back in a sec."

As we stepped onto Daniel's porch, he turned to me.

"Thanks for bringing me along today," he said. "Someday, when you're a world-famous cellist, I can say I knew you when."

I laughed. "Thank *you* for coming. For keeping me sane, for practicing with me last night, for making me that pumpkin spice latte, for"—I shrugged—"everything." I threw my arms around him, hugging him tightly.

But when I moved to step away, he seemed reluctant to let go. He brought his forehead to mine and I felt my knees weaken. "Nadi?" he whispered softly. "Do you ever wonder if . . . I mean, do you ever feel like you and I are . . . ?"

Omigod, I thought, *is this it? Has he been reading my mind? Does he know what's in my heart that I don't have the courage to say?* "What?" I whispered back, then waited breathlessly, hoping, wishing.

He blushed furiously, looking so uncharacteristically unsure of himself that I blushed *for* him. "Never mind," he said softly. "I'm delirious." He shook his head like he was talking himself out of whatever he'd been about to say. "I, um, should go," he added.

I nodded as a flutter of happiness rose inside of me. *He feels it, too*, I thought. *This new thing between us.* Daniel Dae Cho, the most confident, spontaneous person I'd ever met, was nervous about telling *me* how he felt. It was adorable, and made him look even more maddeningly cute as he waved to me before turning to go inside his house.

I barely waited for the door's click before I was bounding off the porch steps, phone in hand, calling Elle. I knew what I needed to do. It would mean putting myself out there, risking rejection. For once, though, I was going to forget caution, calendars, and every other organized cell in my body. Life was too short to do anything else but to take giant leaps of faith every now and then, especially for people you truly cared for.

"Did you get in?" Elle shrieked into the phone when she answered.

"Not yet," I replied after my ear stopped ringing. "That's not why I'm calling. I need you and Brandon to meet me tomorrow after school at the entrance to the Pumpkin Blaze."

"What? Why?"

"I have a plan, but I need your help." I smiled as I climbed back into Dad's car. "Operation Daniel is underway."

Any sign of him yet? I texted Elle.

Not yet, she texted back.

I stood in front of a glowing circus train sculpted entirely out of pumpkins, surrounded by the blaze of thousands of other jack-o'-lanterns. I knew Elle was standing at the Blaze's entrance, keeping a lookout for Daniel. Brandon was stationed inside the Blaze's main headquarters, overseeing the sound and lighting systems. He was waiting to play his role in Operation Daniel, too.

I'd done my best to avoid Daniel at school earlier that day, worried that, if I saw him, I wouldn't be able to hide the nervousness and excitement from my face. He'd know something was up. And Daniel had pulled off so many successful surprises through the years; this one time I wanted *him* to be the one who was genuinely surprised.

Now, heart pounding, I scanned the crowds of Blaze-goers as they walked past. The scent of freshly made apple cider donuts wafted from the Blaze's outdoor café. This Friday night was the perfect blend of crisp air and clear skies; the glimmering, colorful lights of the Blaze seemed to stretch forever across the base of

Killington mountain. There was a field of pumpkin dinosaurs, a ghoulish pumpkin cemetery, and a huge web lit with glowing pumpkin spiders.

As I took it all in, a wave of nostalgia washed over me. How many times had I come here with Daniel when we were younger? Each time, we'd been a little bit older but not an ounce less enthusiastic. Up until this year, we never would've imagined skipping it. This had always been a magical spot for us, and maybe now, it could be again. *If* he ever actually got here!

I shifted from one foot to the other, trying to bide my time patiently but failing miserably.

Suddenly, my phone buzzed.

He's on his way ☺, Elle's text read. I'll text Brandon to start the music in 5. My heart struck a hard cymbal crash, all my hopes and fears crowding together.

Elle and Brandon and I had already made our way through the Blaze's walking trail three times over the last hour, carrying the pumpkins we'd spent hours last night carving. Yesterday, Brandon and Liam had wheeled a Radio Flyer wagon full of pumpkins over to my house, and then we'd set to work. Elle, Brandon, Liam, and even Dad had helped carve the words I wanted to say into the pumpkins. Then this afternoon, we'd brought them back to the Blaze and arranged them in what I hoped were obvious spots along the pathway. Even alongside the other, larger-than-life pumpkin-scapes, Daniel couldn't possibly miss them, could he?

I felt a shiver of worry. Suddenly, a loud warning boomed in my head, like a menacing voiceover for a doomsday movie trailer. *He won't like it*, the voice declared. *He won't like you, either.*

I winced, thinking that this was *exactly* the reason why I never went out on a limb. But then I reminded myself of the last few weeks and all the risks I'd taken. I'd told Daniel the truth about Kiya—big risk. I'd auditioned at Interlochen without feeling totally prepared—*bigger* risk. And I'd called Mom and poured my heart out to her after six years of estrangement—the *biggest* risk I'd ever taken in my life. No matter what Daniel's reaction now, this risk was worth it. *He* was worth it.

And then . . . I saw him waving from a dozen feet away, his

face lit by the jack-o'-lanterns lining the path. Before I knew it, he was standing in front of me, and my heart was toppling out of my chest like a racing runaway pumpkin.

"Hey, you." In the glimmer of the Blaze's glow, his eyes lightened from brown to liquid gold. "Everything okay? I didn't see you at school today and I got worried. I texted—"

"I know." A nervous laugh popped out of me before I could stop it. *Please don't blow it*, I told myself. "I, um . . . had some stuff I needed to take care of. But hey . . ." My voice was a D-string wound too tight, and I couldn't control its pitch. ". . . you don't want to hear about that." I waved a gloved hand dismissively. "I thought it'd be fun to walk the Blaze tonight. It's our annual tradition, right?"

"Right," he said slowly. "But you said you didn't want to go this year. That we'd outgrown it."

"I didn't mean it," I blurted, then walked a few steps down the path, motioning him to follow. "Come on!" Daniel cocked his head at me quizzically, and I could tell he knew something wasn't right.

"Nadi, what's going . . ."

The rest of his words died away as music—*my* cello music—suddenly burst from the speakers at the Blaze's entrance. Silently, I thanked Brandon for making good on his promise to stream the song I'd recorded earlier from the sound system inside the Blaze's headquarters.

I hurried down the path ahead of Daniel before he had a chance to ask any questions. "There's something you need to see!" I called over my shoulder.

I breezed by the ghoulish cemetery, leading him closer to the first of my "surprise" pumpkins. With my pulse accelerating, I wondered how long it might take Daniel to notice the music. No sooner did I think it than he caught up to me. "Hey, isn't this *your* song?" he asked. "The one you composed for your audition?"

I nodded. "I gave it a title." I smiled at him. "I call it 'Daniel's Song.'" Then I spotted my pumpkins and pointed to them, saying as casually as I could, "Hey! Looks like somebody left you a message."

Blazing orange words, carved onto half a dozen pumpkins, read: *Daniel Cho, you are the sweetness in every pumpkin spice.*

"Nadi?" came Daniel's mystified voice from beside me. "What's going on?"

But I couldn't look at him yet. I was too afraid of what I might see on his face.

Instead, I hurried to my next group of carvings, set up along the banister of a luminous pumpkin bridge.

You are the cinnamon sprinkles, getting me through the cold, my pumpkins read.

My face was burning and my knees were trembling as I led him to my last message, set up in front of a field of twinkling pumpkin-carved flowers.

My heart trilled as I watched Daniel stop to read the flickering words on these pumpkins: *You know the music in my heart, and I like you a latte.*

He faced me, and I knew there was no turning back now. I felt exposed but also, once I saw Daniel's bright and expectant gaze, hopeful.

"You did all of this?" His voice was surprised but quiet. "For me?"

I nodded, swallowing. This was it, the go-big-or-go-home moment. I pushed the words I'd been wanting to say for days up and out of my throat. "I wanted to tell you how I felt before, but then everything happened with Kiya, and I didn't think it was the right time." My cheeks were on fire, but I kept going. "I don't want to mess up our friendship, but I don't want to miss the chance for something more, either. Maybe I'm *already* messing up our friendship right now, but I've fallen for you and I—"

His lips against mine, soft and full, stopped the rest of my words. As his hands cupped my face, my breath stopped, too. The world—the crisp breeze blowing, the dry leaves rustling—played a sweet, sweet symphony that only I—no, *we*—could hear.

"Nadi," Daniel whispered, shaking his head in happy disbelief, "I fell for you the very first day I saw you in kindergarten. But I figured the closest I'd ever get to you was being your friend."

"B-but," I stammered, "you never said anything. All this time?"

Daniel blushed. "Um, in case you haven't noticed, you're sort of amazing." I laughed, blushing, too. Was this really happening? "I never thought I had a shot, so I never tried," Daniel explained.

"You could've tried," I whispered. "You're not too shabby, yourself, you know." Then I hesitated, my joy taking a momentary tumble. "But Kiya . . . you fell so hard for her."

Daniel bit his lip. "It was . . . kind of complicated with Kiya. See, when you decided to go to Interlochen, I knew you'd get in. And you *will*. And it's going lead to all these amazing adventures and opportunities for you. But knowing that . . ." He shrugged. "Well, I figured, sooner or later, you'd leave me and Woodburn in the dust. Kiya was my way of trying to get over you. I focused on her to forget my feelings for you. *Before* you had the chance to break my heart."

I stared at him in shock. "That's ridiculous!" I blurted. "I'd never forget about you, no matter what happens with Interlochen."

"I know that now." He brushed his thumb gently across my cheek. "It's always been you, Nadi. Always."

I smiled, my heart bursting, and we pressed our foreheads

together in a way that was familiar and new all at once. "This is going to take some getting used to," I said.

"It'll be like it's always been, except . . ." He grinned mischievously. "Better."

I laughed. "So, since neither of us has a date to Fall Formal . . ."

"We'll go together," he said, filling in the rest for me.

"I can't wait," I said, and leaned forward to kiss him again.

The camera flash popped in our eyes as Daniel and I stuck out our tongues and struck a few more silly poses before the timer ran out. Then Daniel grabbed my hand and pulled me out of the photo booth to let Elle and Brandon have their turn. It took a few seconds for my eyes to adjust to the dimly lit school gym after the brightness of the photo booth. The Fall Formal was in full swing, with dozens of kids on the dance floor and others waiting for their chance in the photo booth.

A moment later, our photos popped out of the booth's dispenser, and we bent our heads over them, laughing at our ridiculous expressions.

"I had no idea you could wiggle your ears like that," Daniel said to me.

I giggled. "Well, I guess that's *one* thing you don't know about me yet."

"Give me some time and I'll find some more." He grinned. "Come to think of it, I have no idea how you dance."

"Really? It's easy." I nudged him with my elbow. "You move your feet side to side, and—"

"Smart aleck." He laughed. "We do have to dance at least once tonight, though." I groaned dramatically, but he held up a hand to stop my complaint. "Nope, you can't get out of it. You promised your mom and dad a dancing pic, remember?"

"I did," I admitted with some trepidation. "Crud."

But I had to smile when I thought back to my parents standing together on our front lawn, snapping photos of Daniel and me before we left for the dance. I'd called Mom last night to ask her for last-minute dress ideas, and after making sure I was comfortable with it, she'd shown up this afternoon. She'd rummaged around in our attic (which, as it turned out, Dad hadn't even set foot in for the last six years) until she unearthed her vintage prom dress. It was a maxi dress with vibrant birds embroidered on a sky-blue background—just the sort of bohemian dress I could picture my mom wearing—and I loved it instantly. Mostly because she'd once worn it, but also because it made me feel as light and airy and lovely as the autumn sky itself.

Now Daniel gave my hand a fortifying squeeze. "You look amazing," he whispered.

"Thanks," I said, blushing. "You look pretty cute yourself," I added, taking in how adorable Daniel was in his navy-blue blazer.

"Well, we make a cute couple," Daniel said, his eyes sparkling. "I understand why your parents want a commemorative photo. And I'm glad you and your mom are starting to talk."

I nodded. "Me, too. It's still weird, and I'm taking it slow, but I have a good feeling." I smiled. "I think she's going to stick around Boston for a while."

"That's great," Daniel said.

We were turning to go to the dance floor when I caught sight of Kiya, and my stomach gave an uneasy lurch. Kiya looked gorgeous in a royal purple dress and silver heels, her hair up in a braided bun. I hadn't talked to her since Daniel and I had started dating, and I had no idea how she'd deal with seeing us together.

She surprised me by giving us a friendly wave and motioning us over.

"Oh, you guys!" Kiya clasped each of us by the hand. "I'm so happy for you!"

She *did* look genuinely happy. "You really don't mind?" I asked her quietly.

"Nope. Coming to the dance solo has been awesome." She grinned at us. "Plus, I'd never stand in the way of true 'like,' and I know it when I see it."

Daniel squeezed my hand as I blushed.

"Oh, and that reminds me . . . I have something for you two! Can you wait a second?" She hurried to the coat room and Daniel and I exchanged mystified glances.

She returned and held two cups out to us. "Pumpkin Spice Supremes, courtesy of the Snug Mug!"

I stared at the cups. "How . . . ?"

She gave a mini jump in the air. "My dad's putting the specialty drinks back on the menu!"

I glanced at Daniel, who looked as surprised as I felt. "Really? That's great, but . . . why?"

"Well . . . customers were complaining, and some regulars quit coming in." She smiled at me then and leaned closer, adding a quiet, "Plus, I told him how those drinks were meaningful to a lot of people in Woodburn, too. Especially to some of my friends."

I felt a surge of joy. The drinks Daniel and I had learned how to make, all those years ago, were at the Snug Mug to stay. Before I second-guessed myself, I grabbed Kiya in a hug.

"Thank you," I whispered.

"Oh!" she exclaimed in delight, returning my hug warmly. "You're welcome. I guess I pulled off a surprise of my own, didn't I?"

"Totally."

I saw Daniel watching our hug with an expression of utter confusion on his face, and I had to laugh. Then I took a big sip of the coffee as Daniel did the same. "It's delicious," I declared.

"Still not as good as mine." Daniel grinned as Kiya and I gave simultaneous eye rolls.

At that moment, the DJ started playing a slow song. With a quick wave to Kiya, I set both of our drinks down for safekeeping by the snack table, then snatched up Daniel's hand. "Come on." I led him onto the dance floor.

Daniel pulled me closer as we moved into an easy sway. The dance floor was canopied with strands of white lights and fiery-colored autumn garland. Metallic gold and red balloons shimmered all around. Daniel's hands held my waist, and every cynical thought I ever had about school dances exited my brain as I fell under Daniel's spell.

"So," he whispered playfully. "Does this beat our eighties movie marathons?"

"Hmm." I tilted my head to one side. "Those are pretty

awesome, too. But honestly, this . . ." I gestured around us. ". . . feels sort of like we're *in* a movie. And that's pretty great."

Daniel grinned and dipped me backward. "I agree. And hey, we can do our movie marathon tomorrow night. Your place?"

I wrapped my arms around his neck. "Of course. As long as you promise to provide the pumpkin spice lattes."

"You know I will," Daniel said. Then he kissed me, his lips lingering on mine in a long, sweet legato. "Still feel like we're in a movie?" he whispered, holding me close.

"No," I told him, still tasting the pumpkin spice from his kiss. "This is even better. Because this is real."

Snug Mug Coffee and Waffle Recipes

When the trees burst into flaming color and the air
turns crisp, give some of these cozy recipes
a try, and you'll be toasty warm in no time!
Just remember to always:

- Use adult supervision when you're using a waffle iron
  or heating hot liquids in a microwave or on a stovetop.
- Use a clean work surface, and wash your hands before
  starting any recipe.
- Ask an adult for permission before consuming any
  coffee.
- Check all recipes with an adult for possible allergens
  before you begin!

Snug Mug Waffle

YOU'LL NEED: a waffle iron, cling wrap, measuring spoons and cups, a spatula, parchment paper, large mixing bowl, a liquid measuring cup, and a baking sheet

INGREDIENTS:

>   2 ½ tsp. instant dry yeast
>   1 cup whole milk, lukewarm (slightly warm to touch)
>   2 eggs
>   4 cups flour
>   6 tbsp. light brown sugar
>   3 tsp. vanilla extract
>   Pinch of salt
>   2 ½ sticks butter, softened
>   ½–¾ cup pearl sugar

DIRECTIONS:

In a large mixing bowl, whisk 2 ½ teaspoons of instant dry yeast with 1 cup of lukewarm milk. Let the milk/yeast mixture sit at room temperature for five minutes. Add in eggs, flour, brown sugar, vanilla extract, and salt. Knead with your hands or mix with a spoon until a sticky dough forms. Add in the softened butter and knead until just combined. (Note: This may seem like a lot of butter and it will make the dough very slick. Don't worry! The butter makes the waffles extra delicious!) Set the ball of dough on a baking sheet lined with parchment paper, and cover securely with plastic wrap. Allow the dough to rise at room temperature for three hours. Once the dough has risen, knead in the pearl sugar (Note: Pearl sugar is small, pearl-sized balls of sugar. If you have trouble finding it at your local grocery store, you can order it online or from specialty baking stores. The more pearl sugar you add to the batter, the sweeter your waffles will be. You can experiment with the amount until you're happy with the overall taste.). Then divide the dough into 8-10 balls. Cover the balls with plastic wrap again and allow to rise for an additional fifteen minutes.

Heat your waffle iron (if the waffle iron has a heat setting, you want it on medium to high. Please follow the manufacturer's instructions for how to use the waffle iron). When your waffle iron is ready, place a ball of dough at its center and close the lid. Cook the dough for approximately 2-3 minutes, depending on your waffle iron, until the waffle is golden brown. Carefully remove the waffle from the iron with a spatula and set on a plate. Continue the process until you've used up all the dough. You'll have enough dough for eight to ten waffles.

Accessorizing Your Waffles

Once you have your basic Snug Mug waffles made, you can have a lot of fun adding creative toppings to them! Here are a few ideas:

NADINE'S SONG WAFFLE

Top a Snug Mug waffle with Teddy Grahams, three large toasted marshmallows, a drizzle of chocolate syrup, and a heaping mound of whipped cream.

NUTELLA BANANA BLITZ WAFFLE

Top a Snug Mug waffle with one sliced banana, a generous drizzle of Nutella, and a scoop of vanilla ice cream or a heaping mound of whipped cream.

S'MORES WAFFLE

Top a Snug Mug waffle with—you guessed it—one or two s'mores! Drizzle it with chocolate syrup, add some whipped cream, and enjoy!

Snug Mug Coffee Drinks

Easy coffee or espresso:

You can use decaf or regular espresso or coffee for all these drinks. If you don't have an espresso machine at home, don't worry! If your parents are coffee drinkers, they may have an AeroPress, moka pot, or French press handy. You can use any of these to make espresso. Just follow the directions for each! If you don't have any of those options, you can make yourself a batch of strong coffee instead, using a regular coffee maker or a one-cup coffee maker (like a Keurig). One-cup pods are super easy. You can use one shot or two shots of espresso for any of these drinks, or about ⅓–½ cup strong coffee instead. If you don't like coffee, that's okay, too. Any of these drinks can be made as hot cocoa drinks (just substitute a tablespoon or two of chocolate syrup for shots of espresso). Or, as an alternative, you can make these recipes using steamed milk without the coffee shots as well.

Cracklin' Campfire Cappuccino

YOU'LL NEED: a 12–16 ounce coffee mug, a measuring cup, a microwave, a couple of spoons, a couple of small plates, and a handheld milk frother or whisk

INGREDIENTS FOR CAPPUCCINO:
>   1 tsp. honey
>   1 tbsp. graham cracker crumbs
>   ⅓ cup whole or low-fat milk
>   ½ cup strong brewed coffee or 1–2 shots espresso
>   1 tbsp. dark chocolate syrup (like Hershey's)
>   A handful of mini marshmallows or 2–3 large marshmallows
>   2 graham cracker squares
>   3–4 milk chocolate bar squares

DIRECTIONS:
First, drizzle honey onto a small plate. Sprinkle a mound of graham cracker crumbs onto a second small plate. Dip the lip of the coffee mug into the honey and then into the graham cracker crumbs, until the entire lip of the mug is covered in graham cracker crumbs. Pour ⅓ cup milk into a glass measuring cup, and microwave for approximately 1½ minutes. While the milk is warming in the microwave, pour 1–2 shots of espresso or ½ cup strong coffee into your mug. Stir in 1 tablespoon of dark chocolate syrup and stir. Remove your milk from the microwave, and using a battery-operated frother or a handheld whisk, froth the milk to desired foaminess. Pour the milk into your coffee mug. Next, toast some large marshmallows on a skewer over your stovetop or using the broiler on your oven (note: have an adult help you with this step). If you're using mini marshmallows, you can pour them into your mug, and then place the mug under a broiler for 30–45 seconds to toast your marshmallows. USE EXTREME

CAUTION when using a broiler or open flame. Place your toasted marshmallows atop your coffee. Make one s'mores using your graham cracker and chocolate squares, and place this atop your mug.

Enjoy this ooey-gooey s'mores coffee in front of a crackling fireplace!

Kiya's Spectacular Cinnamon Swirl Au Lait

YOU'LL NEED: a 12–16 ounce coffee mug, a measuring cup, a microwave, and a spoon

INGREDIENTS FOR CAPPUCCINO:
> ½ cup whole or low-fat milk
> ½ cup strong brewed coffee
> 1 tsp. cinnamon
> $1/16$ tsp. vanilla extract
> Reddi-wip or whipped cream
> 1 cinnamon bun (store bought or homemade)

DIRECTIONS:
Pour ½ cup milk into a glass measuring cup. Microwave for approximately 1½ minutes. While the milk is warming in the microwave, pour ½ cup strong coffee into your mug. Remove your milk from the microwave and pour the milk into your mug (note: for a café au lait, you don't froth the milk). Stir in the cinnamon and vanilla extract. If you like sweeter coffee, you can add a little bit of honey or sugar. Garnish with a heaping mountain of whipped cream, and a sprinkling of cinnamon. Carefully set the cinnamon bun onto the side of the mug.

Enjoy this delicious cinnamon swirl after an afternoon of leaf-peeping and apple-picking.

Pumpkin Spice Supreme

YOU'LL NEED: a 12–16 ounce coffee mug, a measuring cup, a microwave, a spoon, and a handheld milk frother or whisk

INGREDIENTS FOR CAPPUCCINO:
- ½ cup whole or low-fat milk
- ⅓ cup Libby's canned pumpkin pie mix
- ½ cup strong brewed coffee or 1–2 shots espresso
- Reddi-wip or whipped cream
- 1/16 tsp. pumpkin pie spice

DIRECTIONS:
Pour ½ cup milk into a glass measuring cup, along with ⅓ cup of Libby's canned pumpkin pie mix. Microwave for approximately 1½ minutes, stirring the mixture every 30 seconds until the milk and pumpkin are hot and well blended. While the milk is warming in the microwave, pour 1–2 shots of espresso or ½ cup strong coffee into your mug. Remove your milk from the microwave, and using a battery-operated frother or a handheld whisk, froth the milk/pumpkin mixture to desired foaminess. Pour the milk into your coffee mug. Garnish with a heaping mountain of whipped cream (if it's the right time of year, you may even be able to find pumpkin-flavored whipped cream), and a sprinkling of pumpkin pie spice.

Snuggle up with this coffee after a day of hayrides and pumpkin-carving!

More Delicious Treats from
Suzanne Nelson

Homeschooled Amelia can't wait to start regular school for the first time . . . but the transition is much harder than she imagined. Everything about her seems wrong, from her clothes to her hobbies. So when Amelia starts to volunteer at an alpaca ranch, she's overjoyed to be doing something she's good at—taking care of animals. But when the alpacas are put in mortal peril, can Amelia save the only place that's ever felt like home?

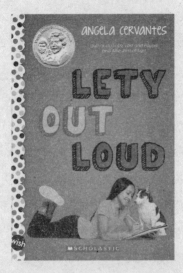

Since Lety's first language is Spanish, she loves volunteering at the Furry Friends Animal Shelter, where the pets don't care if she can't find the right word. When the shelter needs someone to write animal profiles, Lety jumps at the chance. Grumpy classmate Hunter also wants to write profiles, so he devises a secret competition between them. But if the shelter finds out about the contest, will Lety be allowed to adopt her favorite dog?

Have you read all the (wish) books?

- [ ] *Clementine for Christmas* by Daphne Benedis-Grab
- [ ] *Carols and Crushes* by Natalie Blitt
- [ ] *Snow One Like You* by Natalie Blitt
- [ ] *Allie, First at Last* by Angela Cervantes
- [ ] *Gaby, Lost and Found* by Angela Cervantes
- [ ] *Lety Out Loud* by Angela Cervantes
- [ ] *Alpaca My Bags* by Jenny Goebel
- [ ] *Sit, Stay, Love* by J. J. Howard
- [ ] *Pugs and Kisses* by J. J. Howard
- [ ] *Pugs in a Blanket* by J. J. Howard
- [ ] *The Love Pug* by J. J. Howard
- [ ] *The Boy Project* by Kami Kinard
- [ ] *Best Friend Next Door* by Carolyn Mackler
- [ ] *11 Birthdays* by Wendy Mass
- [ ] *Finally* by Wendy Mass
- [ ] *13 Gifts* by Wendy Mass
- [ ] *The Last Present* by Wendy Mass
- [ ] *Graceful* by Wendy Mass
- [ ] *Twice Upon a Time: Beauty and the Beast, the Only One Who Didn't Run Away* by Wendy Mass
- [ ] *Twice Upon a Time: Rapunzel, the One with All the Hair* by Wendy Mass

Read the latest  wish books!